HOLLOW HEART

ROCK HIS WORLD
BOOK ONE

EVIE RILEY

Hollow Heart
Rock His World, Book One
Copyright © 2025
Evie Riley
ISBN: 978-1-77357-739-5
978-1-77357-740-1
Published by Naughty Nights Press LLC
Cover Art By Willsin Rowe

CHAPTER 1

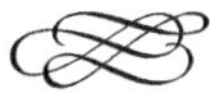

DUNCAN

"FUCK," I curse, as the sounds of blazing horns and road rage surround me on the highway. I've been sitting in this damn traffic for at least thirty minutes, though it feels like hours.

This is why I moved from the damn city.

Glancing at the radio, I note it's been only two minutes since I last checked, hoping some-how, some way, I can turn this car into a damn DeLorean and transport myself to the high-rise where Lou, my former manager, is waiting for me.

Of all days to be late, why today?

I sigh, feeling like things are beyond hopeless at this point. The radio cuts in and out, static filtering through the familiar tune I'd know even if this was the apocalypse and the radio was Morse Code.

Lovin' On The Run. Hollow Pointe's biggest fucking hit.

I fight to turn the radio up, not because it's chintzy, but because *Lovin' On The Run* is practically ingrained in my psyche, despite the fact I haven't played the tune in damn near thirty years.

The horns around me continue to sing a symphony as I sigh in defeat, the sun heating up my exposed arm hanging out of my truck window.

"Come on!" I yell, into the melody of curses and beeps, as if it'll make a lick of a difference.

I grab my phone from the cup holder, swiping up to see if Lou's read my last text yet, the one where I mentioned I was running late.

That was an hour ago.

At this rate, I'm going to get to the office and Lou's going to be a skeleton peeking out through the blinds.

Don't be such a pessimist, Marci would say.

Well, if she were here, that is. She was always so much more optimistic than me.

I sigh, letting my hand slide down the steering wheel, my heart aching at the thought of her. It's been ten years already since she passed. I'll be the first to admit life was so much... easier when she was alive.

Even though there were still struggles, nothing seemed out of reach. With Marci, everything was okay because we had each other, and we had our son. That was all we ever really needed.

The car in front of me finally moves, and I breathe a sigh of relief as I take my foot off the brake.

Maybe I'll get to the office before Lou decomposes completely.

THE CITY HAS NO LIFE, no vibrancy. Everything is sleek and shiny, devoid of color, and I almost feel like this audition is a waste of time because I've been so far removed from the music business for years.

Well, as far as performing goes. I've written a

bunch of songs over the years for some of Lou's clients, but that's a lot different from showing up for rehearsals and touring.

My heart twists at the thought of touring. Of leaving my son.

I know the kid is old enough to take care of himself, and my sister-in-law would be more than happy to come stay with him while I do what I need to. But I've never been away from my kid since he was born, and the very thought of spending time away from him makes me feel homesick already.

Not that he's interested in hanging out with me much now that's he's sixteen, and everything else in the world is cooler than me.

Still, with Bobby starting to look at all these big colleges, I know I need this gig.

When I finally get to the office, I shoot Lou a text.

I'm here!

Within an instant, he texts back.

Take the elevator to the 4th floor. I'll meet you.

I breathe a sigh of relief that he did indeed see my text. I straighten out my clothes, adjusting myself in the parking lot, attempting to shake out the anxiety, the nerves.

I haven't felt this nervous since *Hollow Pointe* auditioned for Virgin Records back in the day.

I crack my neck as I head in through the glass door. The office itself is all wood and black stone, the walls decorated with posters of all the top acts that are part of the *Pillars of Rock* tour.

I don't really listen to much modern rock, and Bobby's more of a Gaga fan, so I can't say I'm familiar with the bands. Though with names like *Mage of Mercy, Heart Killer, Gravedigger,* and *Felix Hart,* I can only imagine they are into all that screaming nonsense.

The elevator takes forever, or so it feels. I tap my foot impatiently, if only to try and quiet the sudden nerves.

I've played for millions of people before; surely I can handle Lou and a roomful of corporate assholes.

Finally the elevator chimes, and I let out a deep breath.

Here goes nothing.

"Duncan! So good to see you!" Lou says, his voice genuine. Time has definitely caught up to the both of us.

While I'll always think of Lou as the young and slender manager with hair that would have rivaled Sebastian Bach in his day, I can't say he doesn't look impressive in his navy suit, with some extra pounds.

I wrap my arms around him and hug him tight.

It's been years since I've seen the guy, and instantly, all the memories come flooding back.

Memories of parties and shows, of alcohol, and sex.

So much freaking sex. But hey, it was the eighties; we didn't question shit then.

"You look good, Lou," I say with a smile as he chuckles.

"You haven't changed a bit since I last saw you," he says, setting his hand on my shoulder. "How's Bobby doing?"

I shrug. "He's sixteen. Keeps to himself, thinks he knows everything." I sigh. "Before I know it, I'll be sending his ass off to college."

Lou leads me through the main office, down a low-lit hallway. Like the main office, the walls are covered in posters of musical acts, and even some films.

"Wow, that's insane. How are *you* dealing with all that?"

I stuff down the anxiety in my stomach,

attempting to deflect. I know Lou is just being nice, but I don't want to think about Bobby leaving.

I don't want to think about the reality that sooner rather than later, I'm going to be an empty nester.

A single empty nester.

Fucking hell.

My friends and family tried numerous times to get me to go to groups, to start dating again, but I could never find it in my heart to put myself back out there.

Marci was a gem. There was no one in the world like her, and I knew no woman would ever compare. Despite the rumors and what others may think about my past as a famous rockstar, I don't favor casual sex or hook-ups.

Marci may have been a fan when we met, but it didn't take long for either of us to realize we were it for each other.

No, I'd accepted my fate as a single, widowed father.

All I need is my kid and my music. That's it.

Lou opens the door to the sound studio, and I am surprised to see it is pretty spacious. Bigger than anything I've ever recorded in, that's for sure.

Two sound engineers sit in front of the panels, looking skinnier than Lou was when he was *my* manager.

One of the engineers is wearing jeans that are thinner than a fucking pencil, while the other is dressed in sweatpants and a long-sleeve shirt that says *Save Rock and Roll.* Combined with his thick-rimmed glasses, and his clean-shaven face, I have to wonder if he even knows what Rock and Roll is.

Lou introduces me to the men. Palo, the pencil-jean wearing man is the producer of Casualty Records, which is the company responsible for putting on the *Pillars of Rock* show.

I shake his hand as Lou introduces his associate, Ted, who is working the booth.

"Duncan and I go way back." Lou smiles as he squeezes my shoulder.

I smile at his pride. Clearly he has fond memories, too, of our time together.

The rest is probably blurred out by the drugs and alcohol use.

"*Hollow Pointe*, right?" Ted says, deadpan.

I nod. "Yup. You a fan?"

Ted regards me with interest, but shrugs. "I was always more of a *Mötley Crüe* fan."

My smile fades as the nerves kick up.

Lou squeezes my shoulder again. "Don't listen to these idiots. They wouldn't know a legend if it kicked them in the teeth," he whispers, pulling me toward the booth. "Just go in there and do your thing. Show these pricks what a real rockstar looks like."

My nerves settle as Lou drops his hand.

"Yes, sir," I say, heading into the booth, taking my seat at the drum set. I twirl the drumsticks in my hand, waiting for the guitarist.

"Someone grab Corpse and Eddie. Where the fuck is Felix?" Lou asks, still holding onto the door.

Palo shrugs. "Last I checked, Felix was in his dressing room."

Ted rolls his eyes.

"Fucking idiots," Lou grumbles as he looks back at me.

"Why don't you warm up first, McKay? I'll grab his royal majesty and then we can get this show on the road."

CHAPTER 2

FELIX

"FUCK," I curse, as the high hits me. My fingers slip through the nameless man's hair as my eyes flutter shut.

His tongue works tirelessly along my shaft. The sounds of wet sucking and grunts fill the air, but I am no closer to release now than when he started.

If I keep my eyes closed, I can pretend he is someone else.

"It's your fucking fault," I bite. In my vision, Sully's face glares at me before disintegrating into pink slime.

Fucking bitch.

"God damn it, Felix, can you keep your cock to yourself for a fucking hour?" Lou snarls, breaking my concentration.

I whine as I thrust my cock deeper into the pretty boy's mouth, making him gag.

"You're just jealous no one services your old beat up dick anymore, Lou," I say.

I open my eyes and grab the man's hair as I thrust in his mouth harder, his gag reflex hitting as drool spills down my shaft and his chin.

Lou grabs the man by the neck, hauling him off of me.

"The fuck?" I growl as my semi-erect dick flops in the air.

"Get your shit together, Felix. You have an audition," Lou says as he tosses my pants at me. "To replace the one that *left.*"

Rude.

I roll my eyes, laughing because his face looks like a purple plum.

"And of course, you're fucking high." Lou rolls his eyes as he shoves my nameless suitor out the door.

"I'm not high, I'm *fantastic.*" I sneer, as I stumble into my jeans.

Lou glares at me.

"We need to find a replacement or you will be off this fucking tour, Felix. For once, can you just take things seriously?"

I scoff at him as I buckle my belt. My cock goes soft.

Fuck, I didn't even get to come.

I nip my teeth at him. "I am the headliner, Lou. There is no show without *Felix Hart.*"

Lou grabs me by the back of the neck.

"You ain't going to have a career either, asshole, if you don't get your shit together. You know the label said this was it. Don't piss this away, Felix. Be smart, for once in your life."

I claw at his rough hands as he drags me through the hallway.

Lou is old school.

He's been in the business since the eighties, and I've heard the stories.

I squirm out of his hold as we brush past Palo and Ted. I see a man in the sound booth, headphones on, getting in the groove. Corpse and Eddie take their spots, looking as disinterested as always.

The lights on the new guy are harsh, making his tanned skin look almost golden in the light. He's not muscular by any means, like Sully.

Sully...

I shut down the thought before it can infect me.

God, where did that idiot who was sucking my cock go?

I didn't want to think about Sully and his bitch ass cowardice.

He walked away from this band.

From me.

The drummer looks up, big brown eyes full of shock as Lou opens the door. He pulls down his headphones.

"Duncan, this is Felix Hart," Lou introduces us.

My gaze roves over Duncan's arms, settling on his sleeveless Jack Daniels shirt. His skin is deep and rough, the corners of his eyes tight with creases. Gray flecks of hair highlight his dark beard and around his ears. He holds out his hand to me.

"Felix, this is Duncan McKay, drummer of—"

"*Hollow Pointe,*" I drawl. I know who he is.

Hollow Pointe is Sully's favorite band. He practically idolized the guy growing up.

"In the flesh. It's a pleasure to meet you, Mr. Hart," he says politely, and I sneer.

"I fucking hate *Hollow Pointe*." I mewl in disgust, rolling my eyes.

I hate that they remind me of what I don't have. What fucking left me.

"Okay, that's enough, Felix. Get in position."

I roll my eyes, giving Duncan my back.

"Whatever. Let's get this over with."

CHAPTER 3

DUNCAN

THE MAN in front of me is not at all what I would have pictured when I agreed to audition.

For starters, he's nearly as tall as me, and I'm a blessed six foot two. But on him, it's all lean muscle and sinuous frame, likely from a steady diet of drugs and drinking.

His bleached blond hair boasts a slick sheen at his dark roots, which combined with the dark circles under his eyes and the way he keeps twitching, tells me he's probably on a bender.

I watch as he slides his aqua Fender on, his

chipped black nails absentmindedly strumming as he grumbles something unintelligent.

He's got tattoos from his knuckles all the way up to his neck. The hot pink sleeveless tee he's wearing looks like it's been through the ringer, too.

His attitude is foul, and reminds me of some of the assholes I used to deal with on a regular basis when I was a lot younger.

Or one asshole, in particular. *Issax Perregrine, lead singer of Hollow Pointe.*

And apparently, this Ken-Goes-Punk-Doll hates *Hollow Pointe.*

Of fucking course.

Nevertheless, I am a professional, and I need this gig. So I shut out my own disdain, and focus on the task at hand, which shouldn't be too hard.

I glance up at my sheet music, waiting for the okay from Lou.

His round face peers at me from the other side of the sound booth glass.

"All right, boys, show time."

The light goes out, and I flip my switch. Felix strums his guitar, and I keep up to his erratic playing to the best of my ability. The other two chug along as well, though they don't bother trying to keep up with Felix.

Despite his erratic playing, I can tell he's pretty good, because Issax, *Hollow Pointe*'s second frontman, used to play like absolute shit when he was drunk or high.

At least Felix can somewhat keep the notes on time with my beat.

Then he opens his mouth.

"You make me weak, make me bleed, baby, I'm a sucker for you. You tie me up, you break me down, baby, cause you're a sucker for me."

His vocals are raspy, edged in a husky slur as he talk-sings.

I keep up with his notes, beating out the rhythm, and think so far, so good.

Until the door flies open and all I see is a flash of black.

"What the fuck, Felix?" A gravelly, agitated voice echoes in the room as the door the sound booth opens with a harsh bang.

Felix's entire body tenses as he comes up against this other man's chest.

The guy is also tall, but unlike Felix's wiry frame, he's built.

Even though he wears a fitted tee, I can see the outlines of his pecs.

His dark hair is frosted with pink tips, spiked with gel.

"Get the fuck out of here," Felix growls.

"I barely been gone fourteen hours and already you're fucking auditioning?"

"Sully, now is not the time." Lou's deadpan voice echoes in the room.

I watch, glancing back and forth between the two men.

Sully advances in Felix's space, and the kid doesn't even blink as he gets in his face.

"Just get your shit and get the fuck out of here!" Felix snarls as he grabs a duffel bag from the corner, throwing it at Sully.

But Felix has terrible aim, probably on account that he's high as hell.

The duffel hits a couple stands, knocking them over with a loud clash and bang.

Sully throws it down on the floor.

"What did you think, if you can't have me you'll get my fucking idol and spit in my fucking face?"

Felix literally spits in his face and I roll my eyes.

Kid is way too easy, and my dad instincts kick in.

I get up, jumping between them. I place a hand on Felix's chest and on Sully's, looking between them.

"Look, let's just all calm down and handle this like *adults,*" I say to the adults who look like they are literally teenagers.

They are adults, right?

Felix grapples with me as Sully *hisses* at him. Like a fucking weirdo.

"Sully... get your stuff and go. No one wants to end up with a black eye."

Sully sneers at me, then looks at Felix.

"This band, this show... You ain't nothin' without me, Lixy."

Felix struggles against my hold, which to be fair, isn't that strong, but he's fucked up as is. It doesn't take much to push him back.

"I'm calling security," Lou drones through the speakers.

Sully looks at me with disgust, spitting at my feet as he grabs his duffel. "Good fucking riddance."

Security is outside the door within seconds, escorting an agitated Sully out as Felix stumbles back into the drum set, the cymbals crashing loudly. He tears the cymbal off, throwing it at the glass.

Lou calmly presses his button and speaks.

"I think that's enough for today. Duncan, you can head home. We'll be in touch."

I sigh, looking at Felix crumpled over against the drum set, his long legs spread out, his head in his tattooed hands as he breathes heavy.

"I'm too fucking old for this shit," I mumble as I grab my bottled water, leaving Felix Hart to his mess.

I'm just cleaning up the dishes from dinner —which ended up being pizza and wings because I was too tired to cook a full ass dinner when I got home—when my phone goes off.

I lean across the counter, grabbing it as Bobby flops down onto the couch.

In the glow of the television, he looks older than sixteen, and in a way, I guess he is.

Where his academics are concerned, anyway. He's always been a smart kid, but I attribute that to Marci.

I was terrible in school when I did go, and it was a miracle I graduated.

"Hello?"

There's a rumble in the background before Lou breathes out, "Hey. You, uh... I know it's late, but I was wondering if you'd be able to meet up to chat?"

I glance at the clock on the microwave. It reads eight pm.

"You mean, like, now?" I ask, watching Bobby.

He's glued to his phone and hasn't said a word since dinner. I know something's bothering him, and I've told him time and time again, he can talk to me, but I worry if I keep pushing, it'll do more harm than good.

"Yeah, you know, just some drinks to discuss your audition."

My blood runs cold, knowing that this is probably the do or die moment, and I need to go, but... it's a school night, and I feel weird leaving Bobby alone, even if he is capable of taking care of himself for a few hours.

"You there, McKay?" Lou asks, and I realize I've gone silent.

"Hey Bobby, are you, uh... you okay hanging out for a bit?"

He grunts and nods. "Yeah, sure. Whatever."

I sigh, wondering if he even hears me.

"I'll just be an hour or so, you sure?"

Bobby waves me off as he goes back to his phone.

"I'll be fine, Dad."

I let out an unsteady breath as I respond to Lou.

"I mean, I guess. It's a school night, though, so I can't be out *too late,*" I say under my breath.

Not that I don't trust my kid, but I'm usually in bed by eleven.

"Great. Does Jezebel's work for you?" he asks, and I can't help but crack a smile.

Lou's really pulling on my nostalgia strings, here. Jez's was always a favorite haunt before we signed with the record company. We used to play there damn near every weekend, but I haven't been to the place in years.

"Yeah, sure. I'm heading out now. I should be there in about a half hour."

CHAPTER 4

FELIX

THE CROWD ROARS behind me as I down my drink, slamming it on the bar.

"Damn, Felix!" Jinger says.

I hadn't planned on running into my pop-star label acquaintance when I'd decided to venture out, but I supposed she was as good as anyone to drink with.

Drinking alone sucks.

"Keep 'em coming, buddy," I say through a belch, as hands pull at my shirt and jeans.

I don't know who they belong to, nor do I care.

"Smile!" she coos, flashing her camera at me.

I smolder into the camera, grinning with my platinum-selling smirk.

"Make sure you get my good side, baby." I laugh as the bartender hands me another drink.

I've lost track of how many I've had, but it's not enough.

It's never enough to drown out the voices in my head.

You piece of shit, no wonder he left you.

I move away from the bar, feeling uncharacteristically depressed despite being the center of attention. Bodies slam against me, hands squeezing and roving over my sweaty shirt, pulling at my belt.

Most of them are women, which doesn't really do it for me, but given the fact that I've had a shit day, I'm almost drunk enough to *consider* the idea of ruining someone's pretty makeup.

The label would just love it, too, wouldn't they? Probably slap me on the back if some pops caught me with my dick down a bitch's throat instead of a guy's.

Jinger pulls at my arm, trying to sequester me into a selfie, when I see him.

Sully.

Kissing some glitter-fied bitch who's got her hand in his pants.

I know I shouldn't say anything. I should just bury all my thoughts, my memories, but I can't.

I can't fucking think straight.

Because I'm *not* straight, no matter what the label tries to say.

Memories erupt like ballistic volcanoes inside my brain.

Sully with his hand around my throat. Fucking me over the amp on the side of the stage.

Sully's hands in my hair as he shoves his dick down my throat on the tour bus.

Sully calling me to come over after he broke up with Jinger.

After he broke up with Petra, Amanda, and Veronica.

The cameras flashing as he held them on the red carpet, as I drank myself into solace.

Just once I wanted someone to hold me the way he held them.

I don't even know how I got here, standing in front of him, but he doesn't even see me.

She's all over him, his hands sliding up her skirt.

I think I'm going to be sick.

All I want to do is crawl into a hole and disappear.

I can't even fucking go out for some goddamn drinks without him taunting me.

How the fuck am I supposed to just forget him?

Forget what we did?

I turn away, running into Jinger, who looks just as forlorn as I feel.

Our eyes meet, and I feel like I might literally die if I don't leave this seventh circle of hell.

"Felix…"

"Not now, Jinger," I bite. Her tone is full of sympathy, but I don't want her sympathy.

I don't want anyone's.

The world around me blurs as I drain my drink, slamming it back down on the bar.

Jinger grabs me and I throw her off.

"Don't fucking touch me!" I hiss.

Her eyes widen, and she falters. I know she's been slamming them back, too.

"What's your problem?" she nips, as a crowd forms around us.

Flashing lights tell me they're filming, taking pictures.

I know I should care, but I don't.

I don't care about anything anymore.

Because no one cares about *me.*

And maybe that's why I throw all my fucking sanity out the window.

Maybe that's why I climb on top of the bar, crunching glass with my boots, stumbling for balance.

I scream his name from the top of my lungs,

When Sully hears me, he turns, his face going slowly from shock to horror.

"Fuck you and your whores, Sully. They'll never be me."

My cock twitches and I don't hesitate to take it out, palming it for good measure.

"Suck my dick, asshole."

The flashing lights blind me, and I stumble back farther.

Right off the fucking bar into strong, solid arms.

"I got him, Lou."

Pain shoots through me as the world fades into hollers, clicking cameras, and a blinding voice that sounds all too familiar.

"Christ, Felix, you really did it this time, didn't you?"

I grunt in response. "Fuck you, Lou, you don't understand."

The unknown voice chuckles darkly, but I don't recognize it, though it sounds faintly familiar.

"Come on, Felix, it's time to go home," the deep voice rumbles.

I don't want to go home.

It's too big, too cold.

Too empty.

I twist in his arms, the mystery man, but his grip is solid.

"Time to sober up and face the music, kid." Lou sighs heavily as the cool air kisses my skin. I think we're outside, but I don't remember walking.

"He's worse than Issax," the other voice drawls. "Shit, is he always like this?"

Lou chortles. "No. Just when he doesn't get what he wants."

I spit at Lou, but I'm not sure it lands.

"Fuck you, Lou. I'm Felix fucking Hart. I always get what I want."

I'm throttled up against a hard surface. My shirt catches on the brick.

I open my eyes, staring back at a familiar face.

The drummer from earlier.
From Hollow Pointe.
Duncan McKay.

His deep, amber eyes burn into mine, full of fury and expectation.

I writhe underneath his grasp. His hand around my throat settles some fucked up shit inside of me, making my cock hard.

I don't remember putting it back in my pants, but I'm acutely aware of the friction of my jeans against my shaft.

"Not today, Felix. You get what you deserve. Now shut the fuck up, and get in the car."

Duncan's fingers loosen their grip as he lets me down, and I stumble. My gaze meets his, then Lou's, who is standing next to his Escalade. The back door is open.

I say nothing, because I can't.

Because he's right.

I deserve shit.

Because I am shit.

Lou chuckles. "Well, that's a first. I think you rendered him speechless."

Rough hands settle on my shoulders as I'm pushed forward. I let Duncan help me into the car while Lou takes the driver seat.

When the door shuts, I lean my head against the tinted window, staring out at the world outside.

Images of Sully and me threaten to spiral again, and I shove them down.

What I deserve...

Fuck.

I don't deserve anyone.

Fucking hell, why does it hurt so bad?

I close my eyes, trying to shut out my jumbled thoughts.

Lou turns up the radio, and familiar lyrics ring in my brain.

I'm waiting in the Black Sea

Baby, for you

I'm drowning in the Black Sea

Baby, save me, from myself

I stifle a sob as I remember the night I wrote *Black Sea.*

Sully thought it was terrible. He called it emo.

I zone out as I watch the street lights pass by and I listen to Duncan and Lou laughing, going on about "the old days."

Jealousy stings me, because I don't know what that's like.

Everyone thinks because I'm famous my life is one big yellow brick road.

But the truth is, my life is the fucking Hunger Games.

There's always someone else threatening to take my spotlight, always some bullshit tightrope I need to walk to stay in everyone's fucking good graces.

It's *exhausting.*

The closest I've ever had to a good time, has been with Sully.

But even that didn't last.

The door opens and Lou looks at me with disdain.

"Come on your majesty, your castle awaits," he nips.

His tone pisses me off. He acts like I'm a fucking child.

I'm twenty-three years old, for God's sake.

"Think I'm fine where I'm at." I sneer as I curl up into the back seat, stretching across the cushions.

I hear Lou curse before I'm literally being *dragged* out of the back seat like a damn sack of potatoes, thrown over heavy, broad shoulders.

"Put me down!" I holler as I kick and writhe,

a heavy, large hand settling on my ass, holding me in place.

"No," Duncan grumbles as Lou laughs his ass off while he punches in my code.

"I can walk into my own fucking house!" I say as I twist like a rubber band in his steady grasp.

Lou opens the door, and Duncan all but throws me down on my couch.

I fall with a thud, my boots hard against the wooden floor.

"That hurt, asshole!"

Duncan grunts. "Good. Maybe it'll knock some sense into your ass."

I grumble as their voices carry, further and further from me.

I slink back into my cushions, relishing in the silk against my chilled face.

"Fuck you, McKay," I hiss, as the world around me fades into black once more.

CHAPTER 5

Duncan

Lou parks the Escalade back at the bar, next to my car, which is the only one still left in the parking lot at the tender hour of one in the morning.

My stomach twists, hoping Bobby wasn't too worried, and that he's sleeping and hasn't waited up for me.

I hadn't intended on staying out quite this long, but the night took an unexpected turn when Lou got a call that Felix was drunk and flashing his junk to a room full of patrons, trying to *piss* on them.

I knew I should have just called it a night, but Lou looked like he was about to hit the roof.

I don't know why I offered to help. Clearly the hurricane I'd had at the bar with Lou had gone to my damn head. We barely got to talking about the audition before Felix found a way to steal the show.

Lou turns the car off but neither of us move.

"You've got the job, McKay. If you want it, that is." He says the words carefully.

I look back at him, twisting my lips. "Is this because of my professional resume or because I helped you corral the Wicked Pisser?"

Lou laughs, shaking his head. "Honestly? Both. Sullivan Reign isn't *half* the drummer you are, no matter how he tries to imitate you. The real thing is always better," he says, flashing me with a smile.

I let out my own chuckle, taking the compliment like a champ.

"But I swear, I've been working with Felix for five years, and no one has *ever* been able to shut him up like that. He needs someone who can tell him where the fuck he can take his bullshit."

I sigh. "Isn't that *your* job?" I ask.

Lou shrugs. "Clearly, I'm doing a bang up job," he laments, and I sigh.

"I'm too old to be a babysitter, Lou."

Lou nods. "Maybe. But you're not too old to play your fucking heart out for thousands of people, are you? You ain't too old to pass up one hundred thou, are you?"

My eyes widen at his offer. I hadn't expected figures like that.

Holy fuck.

I could pay for a top notch tuition with that kind of money.

Lou must sense my turmoil because he softly says, "It's just for the duration of the tour. Seven cities, then you're off the hook. We'll figure out a permanent replacement once the tour is over."

Nostalgia creeps into my psyche as I remember that feeling. The vast stadiums filled with folks singing, waving their lighters across the stands.

The heat of the spotlight and the rush of the performance.

But could I really pull off a *tour* at my age?

One hundred thousand dollars.

Seven cities, one tour.

One shot and Bobby could go to the college of his dreams.

I shake Lou's hand, sealing my fate.

"When do rehearsals start?"

WHEN I FINALLY GET HOME, the house is dark, and Bobby is passed out in his room.

I lean in the doorway, watching him sleeping peacefully, and I can't help but think I lucked out in the kid department.

With my past, and his mother's, it was a miracle I wasn't pounding on doors looking for him.

To be honest, I'm not sure Bobby has even been to a high school party, let alone drank or smoked, or...

I smile, my pride swelling at all the opportunities in his path, and the ones that will inevitably come from working this gig.

The *Pillars of Rock* tour.

Though I do feel some sense of sadness and remorse that I'll be away from him for a while when we leave LA to hit the other cities.

I remind myself I'm doing this *for* him, and that good things don't often come without some sort of sacrifice.

Leaving his room, I head to my den, or as Marci used to call it, my *man cave*.

When we'd moved from the city to the suburbs, we'd downsized a bit, and as a result of such things, I've taken over the smallest bedroom and turned it into my own private media room.

Even now, as I scan the plaques and posters of *Hollow Pointe* decorating the walls, alongside photos and instruments and copies of magazines, I can't help but remember being Felix's age.

I met Marci, in 1991.

Backstage at a show in LA.

I settle into my lounge chair, leaning back as I spread my legs out, swiveling in the office chair.

Despite picking up a wasted Felix, the night hadn't been without its charms. I don't really talk to my former bandmates, since most of them moved away and had their own lives and issues to deal with, so it really was nice to just catch up and reminisce with Lou.

Isaax is on wife number four, and Randall, our former bassist, is tied up with his acting career. Even our second guitarist is still in Hollywood, working as a sound producer and composer.

Out of the band, I am the only one who actually settled down and made a family.

With one of our groupies, no less.

My mind wanders as I remember the height of it all.

The haze of alcohol and drugs always felt good at the time, and I won't deny I still think about some of those crazy nights.

The sex was phenomenal. I did things drunk I'd never do sober, something Marci always reminded me of when we celebrated our anniversary.

"Careful, baby, or we might end up with a repeat of Tucson of '92."

I laughed, remembering her irking me over a glass of wine.

That night, we'd all been wasted as fuck, including Lou, who was Issax's main supplier at the time.

I'd never been into the pills, like Issax, but Lou insisted whatever it was we took would make sex like a fucking kaleidoscope.

He was right, by the way. I'd never felt like such a badass, despite being wasted off my ass.

So wasted I'd fucked the lead singer of my band, while he fucked my girlfriend.

I run a hand over my face, my cock twitching as the memories filled me.

Marci's moans as Issax pounded her into the sheets, Randall and a couple groupies slurping each other just inches away from us.

The feel of his sweaty, clammy skin underneath my palms, the way he took me, arching himself back on my cock like he liked it.

I liked it, even though I never told him that. But I supposed, that was the drugs and the vodka talking.

I grab my cock, trying to stifle the memory along with my sudden hardness, but it's no use.

I sigh in exasperation, knowing full well I did this to myself, and there's only one way to quiet the snake.

I ease my hand into my pants as I close my eyes, and let the memory fill me, let myself reminisce.

I've had a lot of sex in my fifty-five years of life, but I swear that night... that was the pinnacle. For both of us.

Afterward, when I woke up the next day, I felt hungover as shit, but I wasn't embarrassed.

Issax wanted to forget about it, and I didn't have the heart to argue with him. I didn't think it mattered, since it was a one time thing, and we were all off our rockers.

I told him it didn't mean anything. We were all fucked up, that night.

But I never forgot about it, and neither did my wife.

I grunt out my release, keeping my voice down if only because I don't want to wake Bobby, but also because of the guilt.

That I still thought about Tucson of '92 and my wife as my ultimate fantasy, even though it happened over thirty years ago.

That once I could've blinked and picked out someone to service my dick, but now... now, I'm reduced to jacking off in my man cave, quietly, in the middle of the night.

Maybe my family is right. Maybe I do need to get out there again, start dating.

Maybe Lou is right, maybe I need to get back in the fray and find the rockstar I once was.

If I can find him—the young, confident and

happy man I see on my wall—again, maybe I could venture out into the world again.

Start playing more, maybe even start dating.

If Felix Hart and his antics don't kill me first, that is.

CHAPTER 6

Felix

"Get dressed. You've got *The Morning Rise* interview in two hours," Lou gripes, throwing a heavy bag at me. It hits me right in the stomach, which makes me feel a bit queasy.

I open my eyes, blinking through the bright sunlight filtering in through my living room windows. I can hear Samson, my cat—er, Sully's cat—meowing in the distance as Lou curses something about pesky felines.

My hands settle on a newspaper on top of the bag, and my eyes widen upon the headline.

Felix Hart Assaults Bandmate.

Immediately, the events of last night come crawling back to my brain. Remembering drinking with Jinger. Seeing Sully and some fucking fan or groupie...

My head throbs as I groan.

I pull the heavy bag off of me, peering in to see brand new clothes with the tags still on them.

I sigh, throwing them on the floor. My head is killing me something fierce.

"Do you have to fucking yell?" I grumble as I sit up.

Lou scoffs, waving a tuna can lid at me. "Your little stunt last night could have been a lot worse had Duncan and I not gotten there in time."

I shoot him a glare, realizing his words a second too late.

Wait, Duncan was there?

The drummer from the audition?

I rack my brain, trying to remember everything. I vaguely remember him and Lou tossing my ass in the car.

Remember strong, sturdy hands slinging me over their shoulder like I was a fucking toddler.

I sneer at him as he walks over to my fridge, his back turned to me.

"Yeah, well, maybe Sully deserved it," I hiss.

Lou sighs, pushing the open can of tuna to Samson, who stares at him judgmentally.

"You are making yourself look like the bad guy, Felix. Do you want to be the bad guy?"

Lou turns to me, raising an eyebrow as he opens a fresh bottle of water from the fridge.

He doesn't even offer me anything.

Rude.

This is my fucking house he's prancing around in.

"No," I gruffly respond, running a hand over my face.

"Then get a fucking shower, get dressed, and let's go control the fucking narrative, as usual."

THE SPOTLIGHTS of *The Morning Rise* are ruthless. I swear the damn show channels rays directly from the sun, just to make their guests uncomfortable.

I shift on the couch, trying to get comfortable in the black tailored pants the stylists put my ass in, but they are too hot, too loose for my liking.

This is why I prefer to dress myself, but no. Lou said I needed to look polite. Like someone who doesn't show his cock to a roomful of strangers, obviously.

Combined with my hot pink button down, I feel like an absolute clown, but at least he didn't fight me when I rolled the sleeves up to my elbows, so I could look more like me instead of some fucking asshole in a suit.

Give me a pair of ripped jeans and a tee shirt any day over this shit.

The host, Karen Ingram, stares at me with soulless eyes. Behind her, I can see the crew, including Lou, who stands there with his arms crossed, his gaze intent like he's studying the fucking bible or something.

I hate press, truly. No one ever tells you when you sign the contract about all the press that comes with the music.

Some days, I just wish I could play and not worry about the production, the promotion, and the press.

Just me, myself, and my fucking guitar.

But I know that's a pipe dream. I'm Felix Hart. Solitary, quiet, and chill is not my brand.

Karen smiles at me with that fake-ass Hollywood grin that all daytime talk show hosts seem to have, and I have to fight not to roll my eyes.

It's been small talk since I came on, and I know the inevitable bombshell is coming before she even speaks.

"So, we have reports saying last night you and Sullivan Reign got into an... altercation over Jinger Holloway at a bar. What do you have to say about that?"

Now I do roll my eyes, my gaze catching Lou's.

The label has repeatedly paid off tabloids to mention Jinger and I, and they have constantly pushed us together at events, trying to sell this idea that Jinger and I fuck.

Which we don't, and I wouldn't fuck the bitch if she was the last pussy on earth and I needed to save humanity.

Sullivan, maybe.

Jinger... no.

Still, the world loved to ship us like we were the Duke and Duchess of Kent or some shit.

Despite the fact, Sullivan was the one who actually *dated* her. For, like, three months.

"First off, there is *nothing* between Jinger and

I. We're just good friends. I can assure you we weren't fighting over *her*."

It wasn't a lie, completely. It wasn't her I was pissed about. It was the second rate Barbie doll hanging all over Sully.

It was Sully fucking *baiting* me like a prize fish, and I took it like chum.

Anger boils beneath my veins as I think over the events of the night prior.

Remembering my antics in a hazy blur.

Fuck Sullivan Reign.

Fuck him to hell and back.

"I mean, am I not allowed to go out and get fucking plastered if I want? This is a free country, Karen."

Karen purses her lips, her entire body tensing in her chair as she looks at me with disdain.

"Of course, Mr. Hart. It's just that..."

I cock my head at her. "What? What is it exactly?"

Karen huffs out a frustrated breath, her gaze just as angry as I feel.

"Rumor has it that you and Sullivan Reign have been having... creative differences as of late. Can we expect to see him on the *Pillars of Rock* tour as well?"

I scoff, rolling my eyes. "Sullivan Reign has left the band, so no, you will not see him on the tour," I bite as I glare into the camera. "Nor will you see him anywhere near *my* band."

Before Karen can open her mouth, I continue.

"In fact, Sullivan Reign can take his *creative differences* wherever he wants. We've already hired a new drummer."

I can hear Lou cursing behind the cameraman as Karen's eyes light up.

"And just... who is this mystery man that you've found so... quickly?"

I smirk, looking Lou in the eye.

I know he'll probably kill me for this, because whether or not he's hired Duncan, he'll have no choice when I broadcast his name all over daytime television.

If there's one thing I know about Lou, he's a master of fixing shit.

The man's been putting out my fires for nearly seven years.

"Duncan McKay," I say with a superficial grin.

Karen nods in approval. "The former

drummer of *Hollow Pointe*? Well, that is quite a surprise!"

I nod slowly. "Yes, so while it *sucks* that Sullivan Reign has decided to move on from such a phenomenal tour, I can honestly say working with one of rock's very own *pillars*, is bound to be quite an amazing experience."

Then I turn to the camera once more, flashing my own grin.

"So make sure you grab your tickets to the *Pillars of Rock* tour, and I'll see you there, motherfuckers."

I get up just as the camera crew curses, knowing they didn't have enough time to bleep me out on the air.

Karen scrambles behind me and people run every which way like chickens with their heads cut off, but I don't give a shit.

Fucking Karen thinks she can sit there and talk to me like a damn child, she's got another think coming.

"Felix, you were amazing up there!" A voice stops me in my track, just before I get to my dressing room. Lou is hot on my tail, and I don't want to hear his snide comments about how I'm such a dumbass right now.

The woman who stands in front of me is cute, by conventional standards. She's short, curvy, and has poker-straight blonde hair with a spray tan to match, just like Sully prefers.

A part of me wonders if she's been in his bed, but that only makes me angrier.

I sneer at her, as she looks up at me with big doe eyes, like I'm a fucking messiah or some shit.

All obsessed fans have the same look. Like they're just self-sacrificial lambs throwing themselves at you to be slaughtered.

Which gives me an idea, as I see Lou pushing past a cameraman.

"Thanks, doll. But we both know why you're really here, so let's cut the shit. I have about five minutes before my manager rips me a new asshole, and I'd like to spend those next five minutes coming down your throat. *Capisce?*"

I force a grin. I know she'll submit, they always do.

Anything to get in my fucking pants, so they can gossip to their friends and anyone who will listen that they sucked off a famous rockstar.

Her cheeks redden, but she nods as I open my dressing room door, pulling us inside.

"On your knees," I command, wasting no

time. She drops like a hot potato as I unbuckle my belt, unzip the zipper.

Pulling out my cock, I chuckle to myself, thinking about what a difference twelve hours makes.

I close my eyes, and I pretend she's someone else.

Someone with dark features, a deep growl. Someone who can throw me around like the piece of shit I am and make me *submit*.

Someone who can fucking punish me.

Anger over my former lover mingles with my need for release. I prefer to do this high, but Lou didn't leave me much time to piss around before we left, which I'm sure was his intent. He needed me sober for this interview.

I thrust my cock into the back of her throat and she gags, the sound spurring me into release, and I curse as I slam myself into her mouth, filling her with my cum, just as Lou opens the damn door.

"Jesus Christ, Felix," he growls as the woman chokes and sputters.

I barely have my cock out before he's helping her up.

"I'm so sorry about this, Miss," Lou says as

he helps her up. She wipes her lips on the back of her hand, her cheeks still red.

"It's nothing, I promise. I'm fine."

Lou glares at me as I stuff my cock back in my pants, zip up, and proceed to head to my gift basket full of snacks.

"I'll just... um... it was really nice meeting you, Felix," she says with that unmistakable adoration that's sold me millions of records.

"Uh huh," I answer, giving her my back. The longer she stays here the worse I'll feel, and I want to keep my momentary buzz.

The door shuts a moment later, and Lou sighs heavily.

"Did you even bother to learn her name first?" he asks.

I shake my head.

"What's the point? It's not like it matters." I pop open a bag of Doritos.

"Everything you do matters, Felix. I've told you, we need to maintain your image as..."

"As what? A goody fucking two-shoes? Some poser ass rockstar who sings about shit he doesn't actually do? You should be fucking thanking me, I did you and the label a favor."

Lou's face turns cherry red.

"Excuse me?"

"Fucking Karen was practically insinuating Sully and I were fuck buddies, which we were. But I'm not allowed to say shit about sucking dick because the label has their panties in a fucking bunch. Which is why if I stuffed my cock down Slutty Susie's throat, she'd go tell all her little friends and anyone who'll listen that she sucked *my* cock. That I demanded her to make me cum," I bite. "And suddenly, no one's thinking about Sully and Me. Ticket sales go up."

Lou sighs, rubbing his jaw.

"Felix..."

"Besides, isn't that what's best for the fucking label? It's not like anyone gives a shit about what I want, and you don't care about Sully, period. You replaced him barely twenty-four hours after he walked out."

Lou doesn't respond, which only confirms my suspicion. I'd only been notified of *one* audition, and Lou didn't say he had any others lined up this morning.

I might not be the smartest crayon in the fucking box, but I know Lou, and I know he'd want this all tied up as neatly as possible as soon as fucking possible.

"You don't need, Sully," he says carefully.

"Yeah, apparently I need a washed up drummer from the fucking eighties instead."

Lou's hand wraps around my throat so fast, I drop my bag of Doritos.

"You listen here, you little shit. I know you're upset, I know you're licking your fucking wounds because Sully got your briefs in a fucking twist. But you will never speak of one of the greatest drummers of our time, and my *friend* like that."

Lou throws me up against the wall, which makes me shake, knocking over several bags of chips on the floor.

"You need Duncan McKay to keep your fucking tour in tact. You need your tour to be successful, or the label will consider *dropping* you, because you are a piece of trash that has been riding on his looks and his attitude way too fucking long."

My throat tightens as my stomach twists. I can feel the anger ebbing, boiling with something else.

Shame.

God, I need a fucking drink.

"Now, stop acting like a damn bitch, and get your shit together," he says as he drops me.

I slide my hand around my throat, trying to rub away the pain, the tickle that makes me want to choke on a sob.

I say nothing as he slams the door in my face.

The pain, the loathing, and the guilt rear their ugly head. It's like no matter what I do, I can't escape the truth.

Lou is right.

I am a piece of shit, and no matter what I do, I will never be enough.

CHAPTER 7

Duncan

"You're going to do great," Bobby says as he caps his travel mug.

I raise an eyebrow. "Since when did you get to be so wise, Yoda?"

My son has the audacity to roll his eyes at me like *I'm* the child.

"Please. I was born wise. It's a product of being gifted."

I smile, shaking my head. "And modest, too."

I don't miss how he avoids my compliment. As smart as he is, he's the worst when it comes to acknowledging his own strengths.

But that doesn't mean I stop trying to get him to see he really is an amazing person, and that's not just me saying that because he's my flesh and blood.

"Whatever," he says as he heads for the door.

"If I'm not home in time for dinner, grab some Door Dash or something, all right?"

Bobby looks at me with an annoyed glare.

"I can cook, you know. I don't need to live off of pizza and Chinese food like you."

I scoff at his words. I don't just live off of pizza and Chinese. I eat tacos, too.

Hmph!

"Okay, well, if you decide to go all Gordon Ramsey, at least remember to make your old man a plate, okay?"

Bobby sighs in exasperation. "Okay, okay. I have to go or I'm going to be late for homeroom, Dad."

I shoot him a soft smile as I nod, watching him anxiously tap his foot like Sonic the Hedgehog or something.

I swear kids these days are always in a fucking rush for everything.

I would've purposefully avoided homeroom, but Bobby hates to be late.

I guess he gets that from his mother; though, she was always, as she said, *fashionably early* and everyone else was late.

I wave off to him as he heads out the door, telling him I love him and he doesn't bother to say it back.

It shouldn't hurt, because I know he does, I am his father, after all. But I miss the days where he would laugh and say it back, like we actually were pals and not roommates, which is what it feels like now.

God, when we had him, I had no clue it was going to be this hard. Especially without Marci.

I know one day he really won't need me anymore. He'll go off to college and get an apartment, and I'll be lucky if I see him at Christmas. Then, he'll meet a nice girl and spend all his time with her, and then...

I wipe my hand over my face, feeling the beginning of tears prickling the edge of my eyes.

"Get it together, Duncan," I chastise myself, shrugging off the emotional turmoil. I'm sure I'm getting ahead of myself.

He's sixteen, after all, not twenty-one.

I glance at the clock, noting I have about ten

minutes to leave if I don't want to get stuck in Los Angeles traffic.

Though I'd be lying if I said I wasn't nervous about rehearsal today.

It's been a couple days since Lou offered me the gig officially, and while I've been following Felix Hart everywhere, getting familiar with his discography, there's a part of me that worries with his volatile attitude that he'll find some reason to sack me.

That I'll walk in, he'll take one look at me, yell "who the fuck is this?" and Lou will have to escort me out of the building.

The other part of me isn't afraid of Felix one bit.

Isaax was a goddamn mental case half the time, and the other half he was fucking blow up dolls on stage.

Felix and his petulant attitude don't scare me. But the power of his stardom does.

I never paid much attention to the current rock scene, mostly because I had other things to worry about, including Bobby's education. *Hollow Pointe* was a successful band, and the money we made in our heyday definitely gave

Marci and I a comfortable nest egg, but that didn't mean I didn't have to work.

But outside of being labeled a "has-been", I didn't particularly care to play festivals at Knottsbury Farm or do Comic-Cons or whatever the kids call them.

After my wife passed, to be honest, I didn't want anything to do with music at all. I was in a pretty dark place.

When the music dies, you're forced to look at other options. Song writing was great for passive income, but I enjoy making guitars. Or rather, *fixing* beat up instruments that no one saw value in anymore.

Not only did it give me something to do with my hands, but I found it relaxing to solve the complex problems that came with some of these guitars. My family is always telling me to sell them, and I've sold a couple here and there... but I'm no good at any of that business shit. That was always Marci's department.

I haven't sold a guitar in over a year.

WHEN I ARRIVE at the studio, I head up without issue thanks to the passcode Lou assigned me to be able to get in and out of the building during rehearsals.

Just like last time, the hipster twins are tinkering away in their sound booth.

Lou looks up from his spot next to Palo, grinning. "Excited to have you here today, McKay."

His smile is as genuine as his tone, and instantly relaxes me.

"Excited to be here, Lou," I say, tugging my backpack strap.

I know Lou said I'd be supplied with everything I need for playing, but perhaps he's been dealing with punk-ass kids too long to remember I never play a drum set without my lucky sticks.

Every show I've ever played with my lucky sticks has been amazing, not to mention, I met Marci the night I played with my lucky sticks.

All the shows I played without them... well, Marci wasn't the only one into witchy shit.

Some things carry good energy, and I can use all the good energy I can get if I'm going to get through this.

"Duncan, this here is Eddie." Lou motions to

the bassist, whose long, black hair covers half his face. "You might remember him from the other day."

I wave, but he doesn't seem all that interested in me, but then again, I guess that's fair. I am replacing a guy they probably knew very well, and were friends with, after all.

"And of course, that's Cory, but we all call him Corpse, because he's better off dead."

Cory flicks Lou off. Like Eddie and Felix, he has a similar dark meets neon vibe, though his hair is pulled back into a jet-black man bun, and he has far less tattoos than Felix.

Apparently Rolling Stone said he has fifty.

I take my seat behind the drums, dropping my backpack. As I pull out my sticks, I ask, "Where's Felix? Or are we not rehearsing with him today?"

Lou's smile fades as he sighs.

"Probably hitting the bottle again." Corpse shrugs.

A glance at my watch tells me it's barely a quarter after ten. "At ten in the morning?" I ask, looking at Lou over my set.

"It's five o-clock somewhere," Eddie says with disdain.

"Fuck me sideways..." Lou gripes as he turns, likely to go get Felix, when the younger man stumbles right into the room, nearly knocking Lou over.

"And the star arrives..." Eddie scoffs.

"Fuck you, Eddie," Felix grumbles.

"Enough bickering," Lou gripes as he brushes off some dust from his suit. "Let's get this show on the road." With that, he leaves us in the booth.

The tension in the air is thick as Felix grabs his guitar, nearly falling over. The man is so drunk he can barely stand, and it's not even ten thirty.

His bandmates don't seem to give a shit, though, and I realize, they're probably used to this.

Used to Felix Hart and his careless punk attitude.

But I won't stand for it. This gig may be a joke to Felix, but it's not to me, and I'll be damned if I let him fuck shit up for the rest of us.

I get up from my seat, and walk over to him, which isn't that far. I reach out, holding him still, and he flinches.

His gaze flashes to mine angrily.

"What the fuck do you want, *McKay?*" he sneers.

I sling his strap over his shoulder, and he tenses. I look him dead in the eye like I would a snake on my lawn.

He wants to strike. I can tell.

Felix Hart is pissed at the fucking world, and he wants blood.

But I know firsthand that blood doesn't satisfy the hole you're trying to fill.

"Cut this shit out, Felix. You're embarrassing yourself and your bandmates."

Felix angles his arm away from me, gripping his guitar.

"What do you care, McKay? You're just the stand in."

A part of me flinches internally, knowing he's right. I am just the stand in.

But I also recognize someone in mourning, someone who's so hurt they think they have nothing, and no one.

Strangely, a part of me wants to scream from the rooftop, "Me too, asshole! The world fucked me, too, I get it!"

That same part wants to give the drunk, bright-eyed Goth Ken doll a hug. To tell him to pull it together for *himself*. His fans, his music. But I push those thoughts down, instead, settling on something much less scary.

"I may not be Sullivan Reign, but you are Felix Hart. So start fucking acting like the four times platinum, 2023 Grammy winner you fucking are instead of acting like some tweaked out garage band idiot."

Felix stares up at me with shimmering blue eyes, his eyebrows furrowed, and for a minute, I forget he's drunk.

Because for the sheer whisper of a moment, I sympathize with him.

My gaze dips to his lips, noting the tremble in them.

He wasn't that much older than I was when the fame hit him, and I understand all too well how it can warp you.

This life, it's not for the faint of heart. It will eat you up and spit you out, if you're not careful.

His breath is warm on my skin, and I realize how close we are. The tension in the room is thick.

I drop my hands as his body relaxes, as his fist eases up on his guitar.

And for a moment, when he looks at me, I think he actually gets it.

A moment of silence passes as he strums his guitar, looking away from me, to Eddie.

"We're starting with *Paradise*, right?" he asks with a sniffle, and I can't help but crack a smile.

"Yup," Corpse deadpans.

I head back to my drum set, catching Lou's smirk. When I sit down, putting my earplugs in, all I can do is focus on the music.

And damn, does it feel good.

CHAPTER 8

Staring up at Duncan McKay, I am aware of two things.

One, he's a lot bigger up close, and his Old Spice scent is practically suffocating me.

Two... I'm more than grateful my guitar is between us right now; otherwise I'd be displaying my massive fucking boner to my bandmates and the tall, towering asshole who smells like the men's body wash section at Target.

What the fuck?

I blink furiously, the effects of my alcohol-soaked brain making it hard to focus, hard to breathe.

Yeah, it's got nothing to do with the drummer's deep brown eyes, or his spicy scent that's doing weird things to me.

It's got to be the fucking vodka.

It takes more concentration than I want to admit, to tear my gaze away from him, and try to remain calm.

The beginning clicks of drumsticks ring out, and Corpse dives right in with his screaming guitar. Eddie picks up immediately, as I wait for my cue, fighting the urge to turn around and look at Duncan.

Resistance is futile, though, as I move around with my guitar, trying to be discreet. I glance at Corpse, then to Duncan, noticing the muscles in his arms thick with tension as he bangs away on the drums. I look from Duncan to Eddie, and back at Duncan, at the wet spot forming on his rustic, red-faded-to orange vintage shirt, watching his gaze as he tunes out the rest of the world around him, keeping in time with the music, for the most part.

When Corpse shreds his guitar for the bridge, Duncan slips.

But he catches up pretty quickly, and I can't say I'm not impressed.

Maybe I'll have to check out some more of his discography. You know, for research.

His dark gaze flashes up to me, catching me in my stare.

I turn around before anyone can see the weird flush in my cheeks, and my cock twitches against my tight jeans, poking the back of my guitar.

Fuck, I need to concentrate.

Think unsexy thoughts!

Just as we finish up *Paradise*, Lou instructs us to keep going into the next four of our biggest hits. *Bitten, Road To Hell, Solar Flare,* and *Black Sea*.

My cock throbs behind my guitar, and I curse internally. Four fucking songs. Surely, I can get through four songs...

The concentration it takes to fight the haze of alcohol and my raging boner through four fucking songs should land me a gold medal.

Seriously, this has to be a record, even for me.

When Corpse plays the last chord of *Black Sea*, I'm practically jumping out of my skin. I drop the guitar by the door, not bothering to say anything as I head for my dressing room, Lou's voice touting behind me to take five and grab something to eat in the lounge.

I'm barely in my dressing room before my pants are off and I've collapsed on the couch.

The kiss of cool air against my cockhead is a welcome relief, despite the fact the alcohol has dissipated.

When I'm drunk or high, I don't have to *think* when it comes to sex.

Sully understood that.

I can just... be. I can do what I *want* to do, be the person I am without giving a shit.

When I'm sober, I have to constantly pretend to be someone I'm not.

I've been under the label's microscope so long, I don't know how to be *me* consciously.

You're Felix Hart, start fucking acting like it.

The way Duncan stared me down, for a moment, it was like he understood *me*.

Not the me that the label shows to the world; but the real me.

The one only very few people know.

"Fuck," I growl as I pump my shaft, all of my muscles tightening as I arch my back from the couch.

I screw my eyes shut as I chase my orgasm, my breath catching in my throat.

I imagine large, calloused hands grabbing me by my shirt collar, throwing me over their shoulder like a ragdoll.

Dark and stacked like a brick wall, he towers over me, that dark look in his eye telling me to behave, like I'm a child.

Fuck, why is that so hot?

I groan as I come, hard and fast without warning. I cover my cockhead as warm, thick cum collects in my palm, slipping through my fingers as the world around me starts to spin.

My abs clench as my grip tightens and I hurriedly pump my shaft as I ride out the wave.

I stare at the ceiling, waiting for my breath to even out, waiting for the geyser of cum to stop spewing from my dick.

I can't remember the last time I felt this good after masturbating, especially sober.

And alone.

When I finally start to soften, my heartbeat evens out. A knock on the door pulls me from my thoughts. It's Lou.

"Five minute warning, Felix."

I close my eyes once more nodding, even though he can't see me.

Not that it would matter if he could, Lou's seen me in a hell of a lot more compromising positions than with my own hand around my cock.

"Okay," I call back shakily, but he doesn't answer.

I force myself up, if only because I need to clean myself up, lest I want my hand to be stuck to my dick for the rest of rehearsal.

When I finally finish washing my hands, cock sated and tucked away once more, I let out a deep breath.

I look at my own reflection in the mirror, noticing the man staring back at me.

Familiar blue eyes and disheveled blond hair glow in the LED light in the bathroom. My irises have those LED sheen, a circle of light that makes me look possessed, but it's not the eyes that scare me.

It's the circles beneath them, the paleness of my own skin. The evidence of my stress, my pain.

I look fucking tired as hell, and I know Sully's not the only reason.

"You're fucking Felix Hart. Start acting like

it," I tell my reflection, but he only looks at me like I'm trying to raise the dead.

Maybe I am.

Maybe I've been six feet under for so long I forgot who Felix Hart really is.

I shut the water off, heading out the door before Lou can come back and yell at me again.

I turn the corner, slamming into a hard body that nearly knocks me on my ass.

Just as I'm about to yell at whoever isn't looking where they are fucking going, I notice a familiar rust-colored wet spot, and I look up immediately.

Duncan steadies my arms, the heat from his palms warm and moist.

Up close like this, after everything that's happened this morning, I'm not one hundred percent certain I'm not going to pop another fucking boner right here.

I look around him at the sound booth, noting it's empty.

"Hey... uh... Corpse and Eddie left to grab some food, and they are stuck in traffic, so looks like we're going to be a little behind on schedule."

My body relaxes as I focus on his words. Guess there was no need to rush...

"I mean, we can get a few songs in while we wait. Get you to learn some more of the material," I say nonchalantly, if only because I need to do something with my hands.

I need to channel all this fucked up weird energy into something other than my cock.

"Actually, I have to head out in about an hour, so I'll have to reconvene with you guys tomorrow."

"Oh," I say, disappointment ripping through me.

Duncan's deep gaze softens and he twists his lips, the motion making his beard dance.

My gaze falls over him, and he looks like a sore thumb against the rest of the band.

I know we're just rehearsing, but when it comes time for show time, he's going to need to match the vibe of the band to uphold consistent imagery.

I'll have to talk to Lou about getting him some digs for the show.

Not because I *like* the guy or anything, I barely even know him. It's just pure business.

Duncan must sense my disappointment like

a psychic can sense ghosts, because his gaze and his voice softens.

"I probably have time for one more song, if it's a quick one."

I fight to relax, to show any sign of relief. I want to say yes.

Yes, we can go jam for a bit, and maybe I'll feel better.

But I also get the sense that something else is on his mind other than performing.

Normally, I'd bust his balls and *make* him do what he was hired to do, but I'm feeling too out of sorts because of my orgasmic bliss.

I shrug. "It's fine. I'm sure Lou gave you the set list, and if he didn't, you can grab it on your way out," I say as I brush past him.

Duncan calls my name, and I stop dead in my tracks.

"You sure?" he asks, almost as if he doesn't trust me.

Why should he?

I've been a dick to him since he showed up.

I turn, my hand on the handle of the door as I look at him square in the eye. "I'm sure," I say solidly and he nods.

Just as he turns to leave, I call his name, stopping him in his tracks.

He looks at me from beneath the ceiling light, which lights him up like an old 80's music video.

For a moment, he looks younger, and I can almost imagine him playing sold out crowds and fucking shit up. Almost.

"Thanks, for... earlier," I say softly.

In a candid burst of genuine shock, he nods, his own voice heavy with the weight of a lifetime.

"I get it, you know. I've been where you are," he says, and I sigh. But before I can speak, tell him to save his Golden Globes pep talk for someone who cares, he continues. "I know how this business can be. But you don't have to let it ruin you. That's your choice. You want to stop feeling like a piece of shit? Stop treating yourself like a piece of shit."

And with that, Duncan McKay leaves me standing, alone in the chilled hallway once more.

CHAPTER 9

Duncan

I BARELY HEAR Bobby come through the door when he finally arrives home at five.

I'd been in my studio for hours, going over the set list, listening to Felix's songs on Spotify, which I have to say, for someone who's only been in the business for barely six years, his back catalog is pretty extensive.

He's a workaholic.

The man has collaborated with so many artists, released ten albums, gone platinum, won fucking four Grammys.

On the outside, it's easy to see why people like his music.

It's well produced; it's high energy.

But the lyrics... the lyrics are mostly lifeless, save for his last album, *Black Sea*.

The songs there are haunting. The sound, the production, is much darker than his previous nine albums, but I can't say I dislike them. They feel more... real.

I'm in the middle of drumming to *Seasons*, the next to last song on the set list when Bobby walks in and scares the goddamn bejesus out of me.

"Christ, Bobby, you almost gave me a heart attack," I say as he leans in the doorway, smirking.

"Does your inevitable death mean I inherit a massive fortune? Because, if so, I'll find a way to make it look accidental."

I shake my head, laughing. I know most parents would think his sense of humor is pretty dark, but Marci and I had the same dark, dry sense of humor. It's refreshing; it's familiar.

It's our love language.

"Unfortunately, no. Having kids sucks the life and the money out of you," I tease him as I set down my sticks, sliding my hands over my knees.

Bobby frowns. "Out of all the famous parents, I end up with the cheapskate."

I shake my head, crossing my arms.

I know from his bitter tone something else is bothering him, but just like his mother, he lashes out at the people he loves.

Marci was always better at this sort of thing. Talking about feelings.

I can't help that I respond to his tone, instead of asking what's wrong.

Sue me, I'm his father.

A good roast is fine, but I'm not about to let him disrespect the hard work I put into this family, the sacrifices I'm making so he can have a good, comfortable life with good opportunities. Opportunities a smart kid like him deserves.

"Right. I'm such a cheapskate. I took a job playing for one of the biggest acts on one of the biggest tours, just so you could go to college."

Bobby frowns. "Dad, I didn't mean—"

"I have always done what is needed to give you better opportunities. Opportunities I didn't have when I was your age..."

Bobby's eyebrows furrow. "That's not fair.

When you were my age, you were playing shows on the strip, and auditioning for record labels, and I—" He shakes his head, pushing away from the door, and I can see the strain in his body language.

I get up, immediately following him. "What? You what?" I bite, my tone much harsher than I intend it to be.

"Nothing," he says as he heads for the kitchen, throwing his backpack on the floor by the couch.

He opens the fridge, taking out a seltzer water.

What sixteen-year old drinks dragon fruit flavored soda water?

"Bullshit, Bobby. Something's up. "

Bobby glares at me as he drinks his seltzer. "Just forget it. Forget I said anything."

I know I'm at a crossroads. I can press him, but the last thing I want to do is push him away more. I *want* the kid to talk to me.

But I also know I'm terrible at teenager bullshit. For all I know, the kid is just hangry.

I fix my glare at him. "I don't know what is going on, and I won't push you. But, taking out your bullshit on me, talking down to me like I'm not busting my ass to give you everything, I won't tolerate that shit, Bobby. Your mother wouldn't tolerate that shit."

I know the moment I say it, it's the wrong thing to say.

Bobby's lip quivers and his eyes glaze over.

We don't talk about Marci. Ever.

"Whatever. Sorry I interrupted your important *research*," he says coldly as he turns away from me.

"Bobby..." I call out after him, but it's too late. He's in his room, door shut, and probably blocking out the world with his headphones.

Real smooth, Duncan.

I sigh as I look at the clock, which boasts it's a quarter to six. I hadn't meant to get so involved in playing and researching. I open the fridge, taking stock of what we have, trying to figure out what to make for dinner when I settle on a plate labeled *Dad* which is filled with chicken, mashed potatoes, and some green vegetable I can't decipher. But it looks amazing, and I suddenly feel like absolute shit.

Why are teenagers so difficult?

I sigh as I push it back, opting to make some stir-fry.

I'm not the best cook, not like Marci was. She had a passion for food, and I'm pretty sure that's where Bobby gets it from.

I'm not completely inept, but I'm not making Duck à l'Orange either.

I pull out the veggies in the fridge that need to be used up. Some red pepper, green onion, and a dried chili pepper.

I put my headphones back in and continue to listen to the *Black Sea* album while I prep.

Felix's raspy vocals settle over me as he sings.

The waves keep coming, I can barely breathe, burying cities, burying me.

The atmospheric chill of the music combined with the evident pain in his vocals makes me stop mid-pepper chop.

I look down the hall, at Bobby's closed door as Felix sings.

I keep treading water, but the ocean's too deep

I keep trying to be the biggest shark, but I'm fucking weak.

Something about his words hits me in the stomach like a sucker-punch.

I resume my chopping, listening to Felix croon out haunting lyrics about hiding oneself away from the world, and for a moment, I sympathize.

For a moment, I feel like Felix has opened a window into his soul, like he's screaming for someone to see the truth.

Either that, or he's actually a really decent songwriter who's overshadowed by big wigs like Palo.

I get lost in the music as I chop, sauté, and cook up my vegetables, chicken, and noodles.

Once I've plated everything up, I pause my music. Once the table is set, I head down to the hall to knock on Bobby's door.

He doesn't answer, so much as grunt, which tells me he is probably under the spell of his own headphones, or in the middle of one of those online games he likes to play.

"Hey, uh... dinner's ready. When you are, I mean," I say, standing outside his door.

Just as I am about to give up and leave, he opens it, his gaze flashing up at me with sadness.

Was he *crying*?

Before I can ask, he shakes off the look of

disdain, replacing it with his normal resting teenager face.

"What did you order this time?" he asks skeptically, and I sigh, crossing my arms.

"I can cook, too, you know. You didn't get to be a full-fledged teenager without my cooking skills. I kept you alive."

Bobby rolls his eyes, shaking his head. "I'm not a plant, dad."

"Really? Because you seem pretty plant-like to me. Sitting in one place—" I glance at the rumpled bed behind him. "Lacking a bit of sunlight though," I say as he sighs.

"I'm sorry," he murmurs, throwing his arms around my waist.

I have to fight my grin as I wrap my large arms around his much smaller frame.

"You're sorry, huh?" I ease up.

I can't remember the last time I got a hug voluntarily. He must feel pretty bad, and something about that makes me feel bad, too.

I hate seeing him anything but happy.

As soon as it comes, it's gone as he pushes away from me.

"I know I'm not perfect, Bobby. But I know when something is fucked. I don't know what's got you all off on a tear, but you know whatever it is, you *can* talk to me."

Bobby twists his lips, almost as if he is truly thinking about coming clean.

But he doesn't. Instead, he walks past me, headed toward the kitchen.

"I know. But some things I just have to figure out on my own, Dad."

My heart breaks a little at his admission.

I know part of parenting is raising your kids to be self-sufficient.

To not *need* you.

But damn it if I don't want to be needed, and not just by Bobby.

I want someone to need me again, like I needed my wife.

I need someone to want me the way she wanted me. Like I am everything.

Following him down to the kitchen, I take the small victory.

We sit down, and the silence isn't as awkward as it should be.

I spin my noodles around my fork, the sauce nice and thick, full of spice.

Not too bad, if I do say so myself.

I watch as Bobby cuts up his vegetables and noodles.

"How... how did it go today? At rehearsal with... Felix?" He attempts to make conversation, but I can tell something is still bothering him.

"Okay, I guess. He's just, uh..."

"What?" Bobby blows on his noodles, looking at me with confusion.

I wasn't forced to sign an NDA or anything, but a part of me wonders just how much I *should* tell my kid.

Granted, he knows his mother and I weren't saints by any means, before we had him, anyway...

But he is still a *kid*.

"He's a complex individual," I say carefully.

Bobby chuckles. "If by complex you mean a loose cannon, and a total hot topic..."

My eyebrows furrow. "I didn't think you listened to Felix Hart."

Bobby shrugs in between bites. "Sometimes you can't get away from certain musicians. Plus every girl in my class is like... obsessed with him ever since he did that spread in Playgirl." Immediately, he blushes, realizing what he's said.

"I mean... not that I've seen it. I've just... heard about it."

I let out a chuckle as he averts his gaze.

"Is that what you're worried about? You think I'm going to be mad to discover you look at softcore porn?" I taunt him.

Somewhere in the back of my mind, a little alarm goes off. He wouldn't be the first kid to look at porn in this day and age.

God only knows what I had available to me when I was sixteen.

He turns about six shades of red, and his vehement dismissal makes me want to laugh.

"I don't!" he says sternly. "I'm serious!"

I raise my hands in a truce. "It's perfectly natural for a sixteen year old to—"

"Please don't, Dad. I'm trying to eat," he says hurriedly.

Perhaps I struck a nerve. While I'd love more than anything to press his buttons on a topic that embarrasses him so much, he is right. We do need to eat.

He doesn't waste the chance to transition through my offered silence and changes the subject back to something more familiar. Felix.

"Besides, I mean, his music is *okay*... A little emo for my taste, but Brendan..."

Bobby stops mid-speak, looking like he's seen a ghost.

"Who's Brendan?" I ask, because I've never heard Bobby talk about his friends in a good while.

Well, not since his freshman year, really. The last couple years, the kid's kept to himself a lot.

"No one," he says hurriedly.

I nod, returning to my stir-fry. Maybe he's the reason Bobby is upset. Maybe they had an argument or something.

Maybe they like the same girl. Who knows.

When he's finished, he cleans up his plate and mine.

"You must feel pretty shitty if you're doing the dishes," I jab at him. "Think I can squeeze a 'take the trash out' in there, too? Or does that cost extra?"

Bobby rolls his eyes at me. "Fine," he groans

"If you need me, you know where to find me," I say as I put my headphones back in, giving him space.

Bobby nods. "Yeah, of course. I'm probably

just going to, uh... do some homework, shower, and go to bed."

I look at the clock, noting it's barely nine pm, but then again, I know teenagers, especially boys, need a lot of sleep.

Bobby isn't any different.

"Cool," I respond as Felix's raspy voice fills my ears.

When I get to my man cave, I plop my ass down in my chair, and fire up my computer.

While I continue listening to Felix's latest album, I do a little research that doesn't have anything to do with his music.

According to Bobby, his insinuation that Felix is some kind of sex god the ladies are all in a twist for, feels somewhat spot on, but I can't put my finger on *why* that bothers me.

A quick search on *Felix Hart Dating* brings up many people he's been rumored to be dating at one point or another, including the pop singer Jinger Holloway.

But despite his rumored attachments, Felix isn't the one who's been photographed in precarious situations with women.

It's his bandmate, Sullivan Reign.

My mind wanders to the other night, when

we'd found Felix literally showing off his dick on everyone while screaming at his bandmate, *"They'll never be me."*

The words bounce around in my head, trying to make sense, but I can't discern the words of a drunk man.

People say a lot of weird and fucked up shit when they are messed up.

As I click out of an article about Felix and his rumored break up with Jinger, I see the next headline.

Felix Hart Bares It All.

The tagline of Playgirl pulls my attention, not because I'm an avid reader, but because I remember when Issax did a spread for the magazine.

They'd tried to get us all in on the gig, but I was too self-conscious at the time to let anyone but Marci—or Issax, once in a blue moon—see my frank and beans.

In the end, it ended up just being Issax in the issue, and there was no full money shot. Just a bunch of images of him lying naked with his guitar covering his dick.

It was still a pretty hot spread, though, at the time.

I know I *shouldn't.* But honestly, anyone in the biz knows if it's on the Internet, it's meant to be seen right?

I mean, for God's sake, it's in a popular magazine, not on PornHub.

I click the link, if only to look at the cover.

The cover, which, like Issax had done, has Felix standing, legs apart with a bright candy-apple red guitar hiding his junk.

I chuckle a little at the fact that apparently after thirty years, the magazine is reusing the same shit.

Guess some things stand the test of time.

My gaze trails over his knuckles, up his arms. While both his arms are covered in tattoos, I can see the hint of something curling from around his hips.

His haughty gaze stares at me through the computer, and accidentally, I click the arrow. Fumbling to click back, the computer loads before it can register my stupid, thick fingers, and before I know it, the air is knocked out of my fucking lungs.

It's like a train wreck, and I can't look away.

Felix's long, lithe body covers my screen, and the first thought—perhaps the *only* thought in my brain at the moment—is that the headline was much more literal than I thought.

Spread out against black satin sheets, his sizable *tattooed* cock stares at me, and I feel hot as hell.

A tattoo of the infinity symbol stands out at his base, making the long, pronounced veins protruding from it much more noticeable.

He holds his cock in his hand, the veins in his hand in stark contrast to the prominent ones on his rod.

Bright blue eyes gaze out at me from beneath golden strands of messy hair, his mouth parted, skin glistening, no doubt from the oil slathered over him.

"Holy fuck," I curse under my breath as his song-like groans fill my ears from a song I've heard before.

Carnage.

Felix sings about total destruction, about loving someone so terribly, so raw that all there is is devastation in its wake.

His raspy vocals and whisper-song groans mixed with his haughty look and his hard cock in his hand...

My own cock *throbs.*

I hurriedly click off of the photo, but fate must be playing a cruel joke on me.

Because the next photo that pops up has Felix in a chair, legs spread as he arches his back and holds his rigid length up to showcase a sliver of silver penetrating his flesh just beneath the spot where his scrotum meets his shaft.

A fucking lorum piercing.

I swallow harshly, remembering when Issax —high as shit—went and got a fucking Prince Albert.

Though I can say without a doubt, the tiny bar that accents Felix's skin isn't a bad look for him.

My cock twitches in my pants uncomfortably. I slide my hand beneath my pants, if only to adjust myself, but it's no use.

Felix's spread, the memory of Issax and Marci and my glory days...

I know there's only one way to quiet the monster, so I don't think twice.

I shift my pants and boxers down enough that I can free my swollen cock.

Swallowing nervously, I run my palm over the underside of my shaft, where Felix is pierced.

I imagine the tiny silver bar against my fingertips, as a memory from long ago reminds me what steel through a cock feels like against them.

I rock my hips as I build my rhythm, the sensation of euphoria building like a wave. Back and forth, back and forth.

I let my gaze focus on his oil-slicked skin, his vibrant tattoos.

His thick, pink, tattooed cock.

I try not to think about the fact it's *Felix.*

Because that would be weird.

The man who acts like a spoiled child is so vastly different from the raspy-voiced singer in my ear, from the sinful looking man holding his cock, teasing me with his piercing.

They aren't the same person.

They can't be.

My balls tighten, and I know I'm close. I fist my cock faster, letting my head fall back, closing my eyes.

When I come, it's full of relief.

My heavy cock twitches as I press my head against my shirt, cursing myself that I'll have to do the laundry tomorrow.

I fumble for my desk drawer, my muscles feeling a bit like jello.

Good thing I keep a towel in here. Christ.

When I come back from the heavens and my cock has softened, I feel guilty.

Not because of what I did, but because Felix's bright blue eyes stare at me in judgment as the last line of *Carnage* rings out in my ear.

You think you can escape the devastation you leave in your wake

But you can't fight the carnage, baby, because your carnage is mine to take.

CHAPTER 10

Felix

I TURN over the vinyl case of *Hollow Pointe*'s most popular album. At least, according to the record store clerk, their debut *Lovin' On The Run* was the most *popular*—but in his opinion their third album, *Shot In The Dark*, was the best.

I bought all four *Hollow Pointe* albums, if only because when I tried to search the band on Spotify nothing came up.

Seriously, what artist *isn't* on Spotify?

That's highly suspicious.

The sound is unmistakably *very* eighties, but it isn't terrible.

The lead singer, Isaax Peregrine, has an almost operatic voice that seems well stated to heavy drums and blaring guitars.

I swivel back and forth in my lush, red hand chair—it's one of my favorite items in my house —with my cat, Samson, purring away in my lap.

I swear he's the only cat on Earth who can sleep through the loud music playing in my home studio.

I stroke his soft, warm fur as I scroll through my search results on my phone.

Isaax swoons about the loss of his greatest love, wailing like a dying cat as Duncan's heavy drums and screaming guitars frame his vocals.

I get the drama of what he's trying to do, but the way he's trying to portray it doesn't hit the way I think it is supposed to. He just sounds... whiney.

A quick search of *Hollow Pointe* reveals that Issax is on his fourth wife now, and the remaining members of the band are also notoriously divorced.

Except for Duncan McKay.

I stop on an article written in the early 80's,

talking about how the famous drummer "left it all" to settle down and start a family.

The photograph shows a much younger and somewhat leaner version of the drummer who's taken Sully's place.

Though the muscles are still there, visible in his biceps as he stands there grinning in a sleeveless shirt, sans beard.

A part of me envies the smile on Duncan's face. He looks genuinely happy.

Samson shifts in my lap, his tail curling around my wrist.

How anyone could leave this good little kitty is beyond me, but I'll be damned if Sully actually tries to come back for him.

I will fight for custody of this purr factory if I must.

He is one of the only things that actually *does* make me happy.

Isaax's whiny power ballad descends into another high-octane song, and I can't help but focus on another photograph of Duncan and his exposed biceps, his sideways dark glance full of intrigue.

My memory fills in the gaps, recognizing the

same dark look in the eyes of his youth from the steadfast gaze I'd seen earlier.

Though the man playing stand-in is not quite as *toned* as his former photo, and he's definitely gained a few pounds, I can't say he isn't *still* attractive.

It's just... different.

Then I see the search results related to the article below the one about him leaving it all to start a family.

Marci McKay Death.

My heart stops for a moment, and I fight the urge to click it.

Morbid curiosity blooms in me, because I want to know what happened, but I also feel like it's not my fucking place.

I don't know much about relationships in general, hell, I've never been close enough to *anyone* to want to go the fucking distance like Duncan has, so I can only imagine losing someone like that.

But I don't have to decide whether or not to click on the ominous headline, because Samson meows, distracting me from my momentary lapse of thought and my stomach growls.

"Fucking ay," I mumble as I move, Samson

springing out of my lap onto the floor and down the hall within seconds, just as a text dings with the shrill, saccharine "I'll tell ya what I want!" sample from the *Spice Girls'* #1 song.

There's nothing Jinger hates more than being tormented about how her name is so close to Geri Halliwell, the infamous Ginger Spice.

I sigh as I bring up the notification, the sounds of *Hollow Pointe* blaring down the hall as I walk toward the kitchen to look for something edible.

Heyyyy Lixy...

I roll my eyes, knowing from the excessive use of y's, she's probably already at least a little buzzed.

Plus she only calls me Lixy when she wants something. Just like Sully.

The fact she doesn't even wait for my response before engaging in a response is telling enough.

Does Lixxxy want to come out and play? This place is so fucking boring...

I stare at her text as I lean against my kitchen counter.

Hollow Pointe's "*Loose Canon*" echoes down

the hall as a voice I don't recognize as Issax wafts through the chill air.

You're a loose canon, and baby, I'm the fuse

You're a match, and baby, I just want to be used

Go off the rails and explode like a cherry bomb

I'm a loose cannon, baby, and you're a loaded gun.

The words are heavy, thick with a growl that makes my cock twitch. The voice is darker, smoother than Issax. Must be a feature of some up and comer who never made it big.

Samson twists his furry body around my legs as I stare at the screen, at Jinger's photo that accompanies her text.

She gazes up at me from beneath thick lashes, pouting her cherry-glossed lips.

Maybe if I wasn't solely into dudes, and she wasn't constantly trying to lie to herself about her own sexuality, it could have worked out between us.

For a sliver of a moment, I want to say *yes*.

Yes, let's fuck shit up and cause a riot. Let's drink until we can't remember who the fuck we are, until we forget who we're *supposed* to be.

But Duncan's words reverberate in my psyche, like a spell.

You want to stop feeling like a piece of shit? Stop treating yourself like a piece of shit.

Samson meows as he moves away, leaving me to my devices.

I swipe off of my messages, opting instead, for take out.

It's not like anything *good* happens when Drunk Spice and I are together, anyway.

I'm sure if I give it five minutes, she'll be on to some other asshole.

Instead, I turn off the record, order some sushi from Sake Star, and turn on my TV.

THE SUN SETS through my floor to ceiling windows, bathing my living room in shades of ochre and red as I curl up on my couch. Samson lounges on the coffee table, barely even inches away from my box of sushi, as if one distraction will land him some salmon.

I grab my box, sinking back into my cushions as I browse the programs, when I come across a

Behind The Music special on fucking *Hollow Pointe*.

Intrigued, I can't help but put it on.

Samson mewls in protest as I stuff some salmon sashimi in my mouth.

When the band comes on screen, I almost have to chuckle.

Isaax and his long, silky black hair amid his glam makeup make him look like some cross between Tommy Lee and a lost member of KISS. But I guess he was going for a birds of prey schtick with all the black and feathers.

The host drones on about how *Hollow Pointe* was discovered on the strip, and signed a record deal when the members were only sixteen and seventeen.

I blink, stunned as the camera pans to a young, seventeen year old Duncan McKay.

Black eyeliner lines his chocolate eyes, accenting rosy, contoured cheeks. His face is clean-shaven, all the angles sharp and pronounced from the glitter on his face, against his shaggy black and red, teased hair. His arms are leaner, but those dreamy biceps are still on display.

Like Issax and the rest of the band, he's

dolled up in tight black leather pants and a similar black leather vest.

With the eyeliner, his rosy blush, glitter, and wait... is that a *lip ring*?

I nearly choke on my salmon as Samson meows loudly.

Jesus Christ.

Duncan in makeup and leather... with a piercing... He was fucking *hot*.

My cock twitches with confirmation, as I focus on stuffing my face with more sushi as the host drones on about drama behind the scenes.

Apparently Issax was a bit of a hothead.

A *loose canon*, I realize.

As if fate has a disturbed sense of humor, they show the band in the studio, recording the tune.

And I'm surprised to see the vocals aren't some one hit wonder.

Isaax and Duncan stand side by side, headphones smashing their hair to their heads, singing.

Those growly, deep vocals... fuck.

Duncan can *sing,* too.

I reach for my phone, Samson swatting at me as I do so.

"Oh shush!" I chastise him. He mewls in defeat, and I can't help but rip a piece off the corner of one of my tuna sashimi pieces.

"Okay, that's it, though!" Samson purrs as he devours the small piece of fish in one bite.

I pull up *Hollow Pointe*'s discography. I peruse every article on Duncan McKay specifically that I can find as the host drones on about Issax and his antics.

Drugs, sex, and of course, fucking his bandmates girlfriends behind their back.

Typical shit. Why anyone thinks this kind of crap is groundbreaking is beyond me.

My search only lists Duncan on *one* track. *Loose Canon*.

A failed solo album comes up in the results.

Apparently, like the rest of his band mates, my stand-in drummer *tried* to launch his own singing career, but according to Rolling Stone, the release of Duncan McKay's *Heartbreaker* was canceled before it could debut. Issax released his own solo album, and not long after the band called it quits.

I drop my phone, grabbing my box to finish my dinner, noting the sun has officially gone down.

I watch intently as the host of the show continues to show off footage of *Hollow Pointe* in their prime.

Of *Duncan* in his prime.

When I'm done with my sushi, Samson jumps into my lap, creating a furry ball of warmth as he purrs away.

Sated, warm, and comfortable, I close my eyes as the sounds of *Hollow Pointe* on VH1 lull me into darkness.

THE UNMISTAKABLE MELODY OF *LOVIN' On The Run* echoes in the darkness, and there is only the spotlight.

I'll take my lovin' on the run

Across the great divide

Bring you to the finish line just to make you come

Then I'll take my lovin' on the... on the run

The light is bright, almost blinding as I saunter toward it. The closer I get, the warmer I feel.

When I finally reach it, I can see that the stage is not empty.

There sits Duncan, jeans strained against his thick thighs, microphone between his legs. My gaze settles on his knuckles, on the way he holds the mic. The spotlight casts shadows on his face and he grips the handle of the mic, his dark gaze burning into mine.

I'm frozen in place as he opens his mouth, captivated by the one man show.

I get lost in his deep, growl of a voice, in the curve of his delicious bicep, in the prowess in which he *commands* my attention as he sings.

The steady beat of drums echo in the darkness as he sings. Somewhere in my psyche I know I'm dreaming, the music echoing in my brain likely the result of *Hollow Pointe* binge, but it's strangely soothing.

I approach Duncan, slipping between the open space between his thighs, the microphone disappearing.

His dark gaze flashes to my lips as I set my hands on his thighs, feeling the thickness of the muscle there.

I'm well aware that my placement puts me front and center, and I have the understanding that if I wanted to let this man devour me, he could.

He could swallow me up whole and I wouldn't be able to resist such an escape.

"I'll take this lovin' on the run," I sing along with him, as our voices tangle together in a dark, unchained melody.

"Your carnage is mine to take," he croons, the syllables causing my damn cock to twitch.

I slide my hands up and down his thighs, gripping them tightly as I stare up at him from under my lashes.

"I'm a loose canon, and you're a loaded gun," I whisper, my lips only inches away from his scruffy beard.

My gaze falls on his lips, on the sliver of silver pierced through his bottom lip. The man before me isn't the Duncan McKay I know, but yet he is.

He's some cerebral amalgamation of past and present, and uncertain future.

"Yes, you are," he growls out, his hands sliding around my waist, holding me in place as he gazes down at me with an intensity that is both unnerving, and dare I say, intoxicating.

And as his words settle on me, as his large hands settle along my sides, holding me in place, I think I am more than fucking doomed.

"You're early," Lou snaps as he shuts the studio door.

He isn't wrong. I'm not usually an early riser by any means, especially on studio days, but after falling asleep at damn near nine pm last night, and that weird fucking dream, I feel strangely... revived.

Which was why I decided to go for a ride on my bike, which I haven't done in months. Sully despised my bike, not because he hated motorcycles, but because he said with all the money I have, I could have afforded a *new* bike. That I didn't *need* the bike I clung to like a baby blanket.

Even now, his words make my blood boil. I bought the damn thing with my first paycheck from the record company. I didn't have a driver's license yet, since I got signed only ten days after my sixteenth birthday.

"Yeah, well, I wanted to go for a ride. Beat the traffic, you know," I chirp as I continue to tune my guitar.

Lou raises an eyebrow. "Palo and Co. won't be in until nine," he says nonchalantly.

I nod as I strum out a test, making sure everything is good to go for my warm ups.

So, I've got an hour until Tweedle Dee and Tweedle Dumbass show up. Good to know.

I grunt my understanding as he leaves me in the studio and I put my headphones in.

I strum out the beginning strings of *Loose Cannon* since I can't seem to get it out of my mind.

I relax, plucking away at the strings, following along with his words that echo in my psyche, remembering the pattern until we hit the part with the major guitar solo.

Which is not as difficult for me as it should be, being as I grew up glued to my guitar. Friends weren't something I had a lot of, and most of my time was spent in my room jamming out or sending queries to agents.

When I finish the song, I roll into *Lovin' On The Run*.

I have to admit, it is actually kind of fun to play. I'm just wrapping it up when I look up and see Palo dropping his shit off in his chair, followed by Corpse, Eddie and... Duncan.

I pull out my headphones, feeling almost sort of embarrassed, though I'm not sure why.

I stop the music, shaking off the weird vibes as the boys enter, Duncan casting me a stoic, steady look that I can't deny makes my entire body stiffen.

Suddenly, I feel more than alert, almost hyper-aware of his gaze, my brain trying to adjust to the reality of the here and now.

His gaze is not judgmental, but it's knowing enough, and I have to wonder if he heard me jamming out to his music.

Why did I care if he heard me?

Music is meant to be consumed and enjoyed, so why do I feel so on the spot all of a sudden?

Eddie and Corpse take their spots, grunting their greetings at me. I can tell by the bags under Corpse's eyes, he's had a long night, but no one seems to give a shit if he gets fucked up.

No, they only seem to give a shit about me, because *I* make headlines when I fuck around.

Eddie tunes his guitar as Duncan nods at me with a half-smile.

"First one in the building. Gotta say, I'm impressed." He nods.

I shrug, clutching my guitar in front of me, if only to provide a modicum of space, lest I want a repeat of yesterday.

I glance up at Duncan, taking in his present-day features.

And for a moment, it's almost as if I can see the familiar bright-eyed drummer from all those years ago.

My gaze settles on his lips, and a part of me wonders what he'd look like with a ring today, amidst his scruffy beard.

"Yeah, well, there's a lot of shit you don't know about me, *Duncan,*" I reply, followed with a scoff, if only because I fear being this close to Duncan, he might actually see through me.

Past all the bullshit, all the things I keep hidden.

I worry for a moment that Duncan McKay might actually see the truth, that somehow, someway he could discern my chaotic thoughts and recent semi-obsession with *Hollow Pointe.*

Because as far as I'm concerned, it's just good business practice right?

Certainly, I'm not obsessed with a man I just met who I barely know.

That would be crazy, right?

CHAPTER 11

DUNCAN

"ALL RIGHT GUYS, TAKE FIVE," Lou calls over the loudspeaker.

I'm half certain the guys can hear my heavy breaths like an echo. I haven't gone this hard on a rehearsal in a long time, and that fact is not lost on me as my heart races, sweat soaking my sleeveless West Coast Choppers shirt.

Eddie and Corpse all but disappear the moment Lou's voice comes over the speaker, like they just can't *wait* to get the fuck out of here. I know from the countless articles, that the record company signed Felix as a solo act, and later he was given an actual band, with Corpse, Eddie, and Sully on the roster.

I can't help but sense some sort of disdain, or perhaps even annoyance on their part for their frontman.

While I know I shouldn't give a shit if everyone in the band is kosher with one another, it does break my heart a little that Felix doesn't have the same camaraderie with his bandmates that I did with mine.

He's a lone wolf with a microphone.

I glance over at a surprisingly cool looking Felix, who is most certainly *not* sweating buckets like I am. He stands off the side, setting his guitar down, his back to me.

My gaze falls on his sinuous curves, remembering exactly what they looked like all sweaty and lathered up with oil.

I try to force the thoughts from my mind, if only because I know it's not professional, but also because the very thought of Felix in his Playgirl spread makes my cock throb.

Which is something I'm not entirely sure I want to unpack at all, given the circumstance of my employment, or the fact I barely know the guy, or the fact that I haven't felt attracted to any man except Issax, and that I attributed to drugs, alcohol, and Marci.

"Something you want to say, McKay?" Felix's voice hits my ears, snapping me out of my weird daydream.

"Uh... not really." The heat is too much to bear. I remove my shirt, using it to wipe the sweat from my face as Felix curses under his breath.

I find my breath as I use my shirt to pat the sweat off, finding Felix's dilated pupils staring up at me, shirtless and dying of overexertion.

In contrast, Felix sports his signature hot pink shirt with the sleeves rolled up to his elbows and black ripped jeans, tattoos on display, wispy blond hair all disheveled from his head-banging no doubt. I can't argue that it's a good look on him. The stark coloring mixed with his tattoos, his piercing blue eyes, and his silver lip ring are the icing on the cake.

The fact Felix doesn't look high, and he doesn't smell like vodka, tells me not only was he early to rehearsal, but he is likely sober, too, which I gather is probably not as normal an occurrence as it probably should be.

Before I can say anything, Lou enters the studio, pulling both of our attention.

"I have a proposition for you two," Lou declares as he offers us both bottles of fresh, cold water. I nearly knock him over as I grab mine. Felix comes to stand next to me, and I can feel the heat pouring off of him as he swipes his bottle from Lou's hands, chuckling and mumbling something incoherent under his breath.

Lou laughs as he takes a seat behind my drum set—or more accurately, Felix's drum set—and focuses his steely gaze on the both of us. .

He might not look hot—well, temperature wise, anyway—but he can't hide the scent of sweat and heat. Mixed with his pricey cologne, the scent makes my damn cock twitch, again.

What the hell is wrong with me today?

"Shoot," Felix nips.

Lou leans back on my stool, twirling one of my drum sticks as he sets his gaze on me.

"Well, after your stint on the morning show, it seems folks are dying to hear more about this tour and it's star-studded replacement." Lou flashes a smirk.

Instantly, I feel flushed as he raises his eyebrow at me, because I know that look far too well.

"Uh huh." Felix gives Lou a skeptical look between loud gulps.

I break Lou's gaze for only a moment as I watch Felix's Adam's apple bob with his loud, thirst-quenching sounds, sidling away from him, my hands holding my shirt strategically in front of my unruly cock.

Now is certainly not the time!

"So I was thinking..." Lou pauses, perhaps for dramatic effect. "A late night stint on Romano's show, say tomorrow night? The both of you? Felix can dish about the tour, and Duncan you can dish about *Hollow Pointe* and your *revival* of a career?"

My blood chills, which given my heated state, is no small feat.

I *hate* interviews. I've never been good at them, and for the most part, Isaax took all of the credit for those when we were in the band. Every now and then, I'd get to say something—usually something to help build up the star of the show —but no one ever really cared about what I had to say.

Aside from *Hollow Pointe*, I'd barely scratched the surface with doing press when I was working on my solo album, but since the initial reaction didn't seem to pick up the way Lou and the record company wanted it to, all that fell to the wayside, and not long after *Hollow Pointe* disbanded, anyway.

But despite my ill-fated confidence in doing press, I know how important it is to get ahead of a story.

I lean against the wall, my gaze settling on the tall, lean, rockstar feigning nonchalance as he shrugs.

"Tomorrow night, huh? Seems a little impromptu even for you, Lou." Felix sucks down another gulp of water.

Lou grins. "Let's just say I know someone in need of a favor."

"I'll do it," I utter, stuffing down my concerns, if only because I know the more attention we can bring the tour, the more successful it will be, and the better press we can build around this thing, the more money we all make.

And that's why I'm doing this in the first place, right?

Felix shoots me an intrigued look as he roves his gaze over me. Almost as if he is sizing me up, or trying to decide if I'm just being a kiss-ass.

I wonder how much he actually knows about me, or my relationship with his manager.

"But this isn't about me and my *revival* of my career. It's about Felix, this tour, and the music."

Lou nods, his grin looking too much like the Grinch when he's plotting to steal all the Whoo Hash on Christmas Eve.

Something else is going on, but I know Lou will only give bits and pieces until he feels we need to know the full story. If I hadn't worked so closely to him long ago, I would've found his look suspicious, but as such, I trust Lou.

So, I trust whatever he needs to use me for, however he needs to do it, it will definitely be beneficial for everyone.

"Of course. What else would it be about?" Felix counters with a shrug.

Lou snickers. "Excellent. I'll confirm with my contact. I will arrange for transportation to pick you both up and take you to the studio. I'll be in touch with those details." He removes himself from my stool, slapping me on my cold, sweaty shoulder.

"Thanks, McKay," he says quietly, and my

nerves return the moment he leaves Felix and I alone once more.

Felix cocks his head, some stray blond strands of hair falling in his bright eyes, his pouty lips parted, as his gaze pins me to the wall.

"I take it you're a XL?" he says, making me whiplash from the sudden change in topic.

"Huh?" I ask, dumbfounded.

Felix crosses his arms, still holding his water bottle. The motion draws attention to his sleeves of tattoos, but also shows off the lean muscles there, hidden beneath the ink.

Coupled with his hot pink shirt, his bright eyes, and his pouty lips, I can totally see why Bobby said all the girls in his school are head over heels for Felix Hart.

He has bad boy written all over him, but something tells me, underneath all the substances, he's not as temperamental as he seems.

That the self-destructive Felix is a cover for something else. A coping mechanism, but for what I'm not sure.

"Your shirt size. I'm guessing you are a t least a XL. We'll need to get you some... appropriate...

attire. For the shows, and of course, tomorrow," he says, finishing off the water.

"Oh, uh, actually I wear a 1X in shirts, because I like them a bit roomy. But I've got stuff."

Felix twists his lips. "Uh huh," he says as he makes a beeline toward me. He stops inches away from me, looking me up and down as he cocks his head to the side.

"Don't worry, I'll take care of it," he utters, his voice dropping an octave. The tone is smooth, velveteen almost, and makes my skin crawl with goosebumps.

I flash my gaze down to his lips, noting the shimmering silver lip ring he's sporting today. Up close, I can smell the strong scent of his cologne and his natural musk, and I have to fight the groan that wants to escape my throat, or the instinct within me to grab him and throttle him against the wall.

The way he's looking at me is challenging, almost as if he's baiting me.

Like he wants to piss me off or something.

"You should take a break, old man. You look like you're going to have a heart attack," he says with a smirk as he nods to Lou in the other room.

"I'll be back in an hour, then we can resume rehearsal, yeah?" he commands.

Lou grumbles something incoherent to my ears, which are ringing, and I swear I can hear my heartbeat, it's that loud.

Felix grins back at me like a Cheshire cat. "See you later, Duncan," he says with a grunt, his voice dark and full of torment.

Before I can answer him, he slips away, through the door, leaving me and my stiff cock alone, once more.

What the fuck did I just agree to?

I LOOK at myself in the mirror, modeling off the clothes Lou had sent to the house, per Felix's instruction.

I normally wouldn't wear the color purple, but I have to admit the velvet blazer is actually pretty stunning, and makes me look slightly slimmer.

"Wow, nice digs, Dad," Bobby chirps, pulling my attention.

I turn around, seeing him in my bedroom door frame, arms crossed, leaning against it.

"Yeah, well, guess I gotta look the part. Can't have me and all my faded band tees on the late show."

Bobby shrugs. "That may have passed in 1985, but it's 2023, Dad."

I smile as he chuckles.

"You better be in bed when I get home. Asleep," I say as sternly as possible.

Bobby only rolls his eyes.

"If you think I am *not* staying up to watch my dad on Joe Romano, you are sorely mistaken," he says, flashing me with a smile, and I can hear the pride in his voice.

"I don't need you sleeping in and slacking off. That's how it starts, you know," I state as he enters my bedroom.

I settle on leaving the top button of my black, silk shirt—that probably cost more than I could afford on my own—unbuttoned, because it feels less constricting.

Even though the size is right, the fit leaves me feeling half naked. It's tighter, more tailored, and I am somewhat self-conscious that it draws attention to my not-so-tapered waist.

Bobby stops beside me, wrapping his arm around me, his face beaming with pride.

"Ah, but if I fall off the wagon, won't I just be following in my father's footsteps?" he teases.

I settle my hand over my chest, straightening out the smooth fabric. "I want more for you, you know." I stare at the man in the mirror. I've trimmed my beard, gelled my hair. Trying to look "the part" of someone in Felix's band, and not a former member of a hair metal band.

I can't remember the last time I cleaned up like this willingly, but I know how important appearances can be, especially on television.

Bobby smiles. "I know, Dad." He says the words softly, like they are made of glass.

My phone dings, breaking the moment, and I see that it's Lou, telling me my transport should be arriving any minute.

I turn to hug my son, gripping him like he is a life raft. And maybe in some ways, he is.

I always thought I'd be the one in this position, fixing his cufflinks, straightening his tie before a big date, or even the prom.

But Bobby never goes on dates, and as far as I knew he hasn't been asked to the prom.

"Knock 'em dead, Dad," he whispers in my ear, before letting me go.

"Abso-fucking-lutely, kid." I chin up, channeling confidence that I'm not sure I really have, but hey... fake it until you make it, right?

THE MINUTE I step foot onto the set of the late night show, it all comes flashing back.

Memories of *Hollow Pointe*'s musical guest spots, memories of me underneath the bright, hot lights while Issax went on and on about whatever topic his drug-induced high took him on.

Me, under those bright lights while hosts asked me about my solo career—the one that never happened.

You can do this, I tell myself.

It's for the show.

"And this is your dressing—" My guide and I stop in front of what I assume to be my dressing room, but it looks like a science experiment gone wrong. There is a crew of men in overalls and suits with masks walking through the doorway, with their arms full of pipes and cleaning products.

"Excuse me, what's going on here?" My guide, a sweet, young woman who, in my opinion, is far too cheerful to be working this late at night, asks a passing worker.

I can't help but glance back and forth between her and the man in her line of vision, and for a moment I fear for him.

Tiny and sweet as she is, she looks like she could kill him.

"There was a complaint about something in the ducts, we investigated and found a small family of raccoons."

Raccoons?

"You do realize we have a show to put on..." she growls, her eyebrow twitching.

The man in question crosses his arms, unfazed by my guide's rising anger.

"Noted. I was told to block off this room until we've trapped all the raccoons. So, I suggest whatever it is you need to do, you do it somewhere else."

I can feel the tension rising, so I do the only thing I can think of.

I step in.

"It's fine, I don't *need* a dressing room. I'm already dressed, anyway," I quip, trying to joke and lighten the mood as my guide's phone goes off.

She shoots a glare at the raccoon handler, then back at me before tapping away furiously on her phone.

"Not to worry, Mr. McKay. We'll just have to stick you in with your bandmate until show time." She says the words as if they are a punishment, rather than a solution, and I sigh, knowing it's best not to fight.

I follow her through the winding halls, down corridors, until we come to another dressing room. The sign outside the door reads *Felix Hart*.

"I do apologize for the inconvenience," she says, looking at me with big eyes that pray I won't complain to her boss.

I reach out and pat her shoulder lightly, offering her a soft smile. "Shit happens. I promise, it's fine. Don't worry."

Something in her gaze shifts at my words and she nods. "Th–thanks. Felix's room should be stocked to his preferences, but if there is anything you need—"

"I'll call. Really, I'm fine. I don't need much," I assure her, and this seems to do the trick as she smiles, taking her leave.

I rap my knuckle on the door, but I don't hear anything.

Maybe Felix isn't here yet.

I open the door, slipping in, and immediately regret it.

I close the door fast, with a slam, as I am met with the sight of Felix. In his fucking *underwear*.

His long, lithe frame on full display, including the left and right loops of the infinity symbol that curl from beneath his hips, is like a train wreck.

I can't look away, nor can I stop the curse that falls out of my mouth.

"Jesus Christ, Felix, put some fucking clothes on."

Felix laughs, and the sound is some cross between haughty and lighthearted.

"What's the matter, Duncan? Does my immaculate form make you self-conscious?" he taunts.

I scoff at his overconfidence.

I wouldn't call Felix *immaculate* by any

means. The man could use a cheeseburger or two...

"Don't flatter yourself," I bite back as I begin to make my way to the couch, but Felix stops me by getting in my way.

"Look at you, all cleaned up and pretty," he croons, brushing something off my shoulder.

I'm acutely aware of his proximity to me, and so is my cock.

Up close like this, I can smell his heady cologne, mixed with the scent of freshly washed hair, and I can't deny it smells divine.

I glance down at Felix's face, marveling once more at those pouty, pierced lips. He's got a simple silver ring in, and I don't miss the way it jiggles, telling me his tongue is playing with it.

Why that notion makes my cock twitch, I have no idea.

"Yes, well, what was I supposed to do when a capsule wardrobe showed up at my door?" I mutter as he runs his fingers down my velvet sleeve.

His eyes flash with a brightness that is clear, stable. Once again, the pain in the ass is stone cold sober, and something about that fact feels... important, though I'm not sure why.

Maybe I actually got through to him.

"I must admit, I half thought you would send it back." He blinks, taking a step back, heading toward the dresser.

Giving me ample sight of his back, of those corded lean muscles.

I'm not shocked when I see the wings on his shoulder blades, even though his spread in Playgirl showed a bare back.

"Those new?" I ask, trying my hardest *not* to watch slinky Felix in his underwear like some fucking pervert.

The notion is more difficult than it should be.

I stand off his side, keeping my distance, strategically angling myself so I can adjust my cock without drawing attention.

God, that would be awkward as hell. Surely, Felix would fire my ass if he thought...

I swallow harshly as he jiggles his slacks on, watching his tattooed knuckles fasten his belt.

"The wings, I mean?" I blurt, trying to focus on anything but the way the shadows and ink light up his form.

"I've had 'em for a couple years, why?"

"Just, uh... curious," I reply.

Felix pulls on his bright pink shirt, slowly working on the bottom button as he saunters across the room, his gaze pinning me to my place.

The look on his face is predatory, but also... playful.

Like he enjoys tormenting me and making me uncomfortable.

Maybe he does.

I know that should bother me.

Hell, most of the time everything Felix does, bothers me.

So why does this feel different?

He stands tall, but I am taller.

His bright blue eyes gaze up at me as he lazily buttons the second button, pouting his lips.

"What about you, Duncan? Got any ink to show and tell? Something... new?"

I do. Though it's not new and I'll be damned if I show him.

The only people who have ever seen my regrettable black cat tattoo are my bandmates and Marci.

Bobby doesn't even know I have a tattoo.

And he'll never see it because it's on my fucking ass.

"Wouldn't you like to know," I huff, indignant.

Felix chuckles, licking his lips. His tongue probes his lip ring, blue eyes blazing as he continues his buttoning.

My cock throbs against my tight jeans as he leans closer to me, brushing his chest against mine, and I feel lightheaded.

Part of me wants to deck him.

To push him and run as far away as possible, and tell him to fuck off and do this interview himself.

But the other part of me, the one that wins out, wants to grab him by the damn throat and *show* him his place in a way that is as new to me as it is familiar.

I am frozen under his gaze, but I know I need to fight for my place.

I can't let Felix think he has the upper hand, ever.

Even if he does.

He grins sexily. "Oooh, that means you do. And it's probably scandalous." He licks his lips.

"You'd just love that, wouldn't you?" I bite. It wasn't a question, as much as it was a statement.

"Since when do you care what I like? Aren't you just here to manhandle me and tell me what to do? Isn't that why Lou brought you in? To *handle* me?"

His words are taunting, but they also make me feel hot all over.

"Fuck you," I bark, my voice solid as I bump his chest, the motion drawing attention to my unruly cock, and immediately, I panic.

Felix's eyes widen, as does his grin.

"Is that a drumstick in your pocket, Duncan, or are you just really happy to see me?" he drawls. His tone is dark yet playful, like he actually *enjoys* this exchange.

I bite back, feeling more on the spot than ever before. "Not everyone in a five-mile radius wants to fuck you, Felix."

The moment I say the words, I know I can't take it back.

For a sliver of a moment, Felix's gaze softens, almost going glassy, and I feel like an asshole.

I hadn't meant my tone to sound so harsh. I'm not sure if I'm trying to convince him or myself of that truth.

I'm also not certain that everyone within a five-mile radius *didn't* want to fuck him.

Because the way he looks right now...

No.

Absolutely fucking not.

The moment of truth dissipates nearly instantly, Felix once more replaced by pain in the ass brat I've come to know.

"Says the man who probably hasn't been fucked since before the invention of the cell phone."

His words piss me off, and just as I am about to lay into him about them, a knock on the door pulls both of our attention.

"Ten minute warning, boys," Lou touts from the other side, the door remaining shut. "Quit fucking around and let's get this show on the road."

CHAPTER 12

FELIX

I'VE NEVER BEEN MORE thankful to be interrupted by my manager in my life. Because I know, if Lou hadn't banged his fist on my dressing room door, I might've just fucking kissed Duncan McKay.

I know it was probably not a good idea to even let myself *think* about my current drummer in that way, and God only knows why I wanted to, least of all because my *relationship* with my last drummer didn't end well.

That's an understatement. The man saw you

as a fucktoy and nothing else. Which was fine until it wasn't.

I usually preferred built, pretty boys with a little edginess to them, like Sully, but I can't deny that Duncan dressed up in purple velvet, his beard *neatly* trimmed, and his gaze all smoldering mixed with his solid, stocky figure is fucking hot as hell.

Not to mention the fact that he seems to be one of the only people on the planet who cuts through the bullshit and is fucking *real* with me.

From the moment I met him, he's never treated me like Felix Hart, the rockstar.

He's treated me like I'm a just a regular person.

A person who probably annoys the shit out of him, and who will end up with a fist in his face if you make a wrong move.

But then, for the glimmer of a moment, something in his gaze shifts.

And something in his pants.

Fuck!

How am I supposed to get that image out of my fucking mind now?

"Okay, boys, look alive out there," Lou orders with a grin, smacking us both on the back, and there's barely any time for either of us to dwell on what happened between us.

What exactly did happen between us?

Joe introduces us, and I take the lead, Duncan hanging behind me.

Time to play the part.

I shove all thoughts, all personal feelings and worries aside as I stretch my lips into a wide grin.

"Joe! It's so good to be back, man." I pull him into a half hug, slapping him on the back.

Duncan half smiles, extending his hand, and I have to give him credit for looking Joe in the eye.

"Have a seat, have a seat." Joe gestures for us to take our spot on the couch.

I take my seat first, crossing my ankle over my knee as Duncan sits down gingerly, taking up more than half of the couch. His thigh brushes mine, and I have to fight the impulse to set my hand on it as images flash from my weird dream.

The crowd quiets, and there is a moment of awkward silence as Joe sits behind his desk, straightening his tie as he looks at the camera, then at us.

"So, Felix, it's been awhile since we had you

on the show, and I see you brought a new friend with you."

I keep my gaze cool and aloof as I stretch my arm back along the top of the couch. I shift my body strategically to give a sliver of space between us, and keep my hand flat on the cushion. I can feel the slight tremor of Duncan's thigh, almost as if he is nervous.

I'm not sure if it's because of what happened before coming out here, or if it's the heavy, bright lights and the hoopla of being on television after being out of the spotlight for nearly thirty years.

"Yes, I did!" I flash a smile as I turn my grin to Duncan, imploring him with my gaze.

"Duncan is performing with the band for the *Pillars of Rock* tour, which is how we met." I nod at Duncan, hoping he picks up on my body language.

Thankfully, he does, and he smiles a bit more

"Yes, that's correct," he says stiffly.

Joe chuckles a bit as he says, "Man, I gotta say this is a dream come true. I was always a *huge* fan of *Hollow Pointe* growing up. I think I actually went as Issax one year for Halloween, as a kid."

I chuckle to myself, even though it's not

genuine, but the audience plays right along, like they always do.

"Although, I can imagine it's got to be somewhat difficult for you, Felix, playing with someone so talented. I mean, Duncan, you are a literal legend!"

Duncan looks uncomfortable as hell with the compliment, like instead of being called a pillar of rock himself, Joe just insulted him or something, but he brushes it off.

"Oh, for sure. Duncan definitely keeps me on my toes, don't you Duncan?" I smirk, and his eyebrows narrow at me.

"That's right. There's definitely a thing or two I can teach you."

I half laugh, half gasp at his playful tone. The audience and Joe both laugh along with him. He grins, but it isn't genuine.

In fact, it's deadly, and it makes my heart beat a little faster.

Joe ooohs as the audience coos along with him, at Duncan's sizzling comeback.

I shift my stance, regaling him with my own gaze.

"Yes, well, if I need to learn how to operate a VCR, I'll be sure to give you a call," I return with a smirk. "I hear those are starting to become all the rage nowadays. Sometimes I feel like there's a poetry to watching those poor pixels, and the fuzziness, you know, in a world of digitization and streaming. I swear there's something magical about the phrase, 'please be kind rewind.'"

Joe doesn't miss a beat, and I can hear the slight shift in his tone, like he's not sure if Duncan and I won't get into a damn brawl right here.

And I guess, I sort of understand. I don't exactly have the best track record. I did get into a fight once with Jared Leto backstage.

And you were just seen publicly beefing with Sully.

Duncan shifts his stance, which pushes my right asscheek off the couch altogether.

Touche, Duncan.

"Everything comes back around, if you're around long enough." Duncan shrugs.

"True that," Joe replies as he focus his gaze on me.

"There have been a ton of rumors flying about lately about the state of your band, Felix. It was reported a week ago that you and Sullivan Reign have disbanded your... partnership?"

My blood chills at his words, because even for him, it's a low blow.

We both know what he's asking, what can't be said on air, or in the public at all.

I'm irritated at his question, but I know it's what he does. All these talk show hosts are the same. They say their job is the news, but it's not. It's gossip.

The Joe's, the Karen's, the Channel 5 reporter, and the paparazzi... they are all the same. In the business of *gossip.*

After all, late night news covers the dirt, and where Sullivan Reign and I are concerned, there is quite a bit of it.

That's the thing about these damn media circuses. They don't dispel rumors, they create them, then offer you a platform to make your public statement or apology on the mountain of lies they created.

Any celebrity worth their salt knows that.

But as usual, I need to keep to my script, keep to the narrative that works for *me* and the record label.

"Sully is a talented man," I start, looking at Duncan, for what I'm not sure.

Back up?

Understanding?

I shouldn't really give two shits about Duncan's feelings regarding my former drummer, but for some reason I do.

Which makes me care a little more about what I say next, to Joe and the world, even though it doesn't make any fucking sense.

"His desire to explore those... talents..." I shoot Joe a death glare, enunciating the last word vibrantly so he understands that I know what game he's playing and I'm not giving in.

"Who am I to deny my *good friend* a chance to explore a... different side of himself? Besides,"

I shift my stance, cocking my head to the side as I hone in my sights on a rather placid looking Joe while Lou and the producers off stage are bathed in light, practically chewing their fingernails.

"I'm a one man show. The name of the band is Felix Hart. Not Felix Hart and the Jackasses." I shrug.

Take that, Sully!

Joe chuckles, shaking his head.

"And the rumors that it was Jinger Holloway that came between you two is just a rumor, right?" Joe says with his signature snark.

I can't help but roll my eyes.

"I can assure you, there is nothing going on between Jinger and I."

There never has been, but the public doesn't seem to get that.

"We're just friends," I say, folding my hands in my lap.

Joe grins. "Right. Just friends. Never any romantic entanglements for you."

I glare at him. My relationships are not what we came here to discuss.

"That's right." I reply, plastering a "lets move the fuck on" glare on my face, hoping he'll get the memo.

To my relief, he switches gears, aiming for Duncan.

"Speaking of romantic entanglements, Duncan, we were all so very sorry to hear about your wife, Marci," Joe says with practiced empathy.

Duncan's shoulders tense, his spine straightening at Joe's words, because he knows what's coming.

And I guess I shouldn't be surprised, but somehow, I still am.

"It's been, what ten years, now?" Joe asks.

Duncan grunts out an uneven, "Yes."

The words hit me just a moment too late, as I realize that Duncan was not prepared for this.

I've seen the articles, but even I felt like it wasn't my place to dive into someone's personal life.

It was more than apparent that Duncan had *left* all of the fame and fortune to build a family, and up until recently, had more than relished his privacy.

I turn to look at Duncan, his face pale.

I'm sure he wasn't expecting the question, and quite frankly, neither was I. That is a low blow, even for Joe, and no doubt he did it on account that it would get everyone talking at the watercoolers tomorrow.

Anger swells within me as my fingertips graze the edge of his back.

How dare these assholes throw salt in Duncan's wounds just for fucking ratings!

"That must have been difficult," Joe says.

Without thinking, I trace my fingers up and down the back of his velvet blazer, trying to soothe his nerves.

It's okay. I got this.

I jump in. "Of course. Losing someone you

love is always difficult. It's also extremely personal, and not everyone's fucking business."

I catch Lou's eyes widen off stage, but the way Duncan's spine *relaxes* is worth whatever bellowing I will endure from Lou or the company for being an asshole on the air.

A small price to pay to put someone in their place

Joe holds his hands up in mock surrender.

"Of course it is. I only wanted to express my condolences on the matter."

I bet you did.

Duncan gives a half smile as he leans forward, his elbows on his knees. He nods at Joe, grunting out a thank you.

"To answer your question, yes, it was difficult. There are still days where it's difficult, and that will never change. You don't ever get over something like that, you just learn how to live with it. You can't let pain define you. You have to learn how to co-exist with it, how to use it."

His words are profound, heavy.

The tension that befalls the room is thick and I can't help but look at this man, his deep eyes as vast as the depths in which his grief still runs.

I want to fucking tear Joe and the producers

of this show a new asshole for putting Duncan on the spot like this, for hurting him.

I speak without thinking.

"Music has always been a channel for *my* pain," I declare, as I look him in his eyes.

Duncan's gaze meets mine, and I continue, steering the discussion back to the reason we're both here.

The tour.

If there's anything I've learned in these past few years, it's damage control. Lord knows, I've needed enough of it myself.

"Which is another reason why I think this tour is more than just a tour. It's a homecoming of sorts, not just for myself and Duncan, but for the other acts as well. Dare, Geo, Matty... all of us are just fucking misfits, man. We all wear our hearts on our sleeves, and that's why this tour is so important. It's not just about the music, it's about what music does. It heals."

Duncan's lips turn up slightly in the corner, his gaze glittering with warmth.

"Absolutely."

Joe grins, and I see the producer flashing his hand signs, a digital screen counting down until we are off the air.

CHAPTER 13

DUNCAN

A THOUSAND THINGS run through my mind once the producers cut from the air. There's a hundred things I want to say to Felix, but before I can, a group of folks hurry him off stage, leaving me alone with Joe.

"Hey man, I wasn't trying to be a dick or anything. I really am sorry for your loss," he says, and I can tell it is genuine.

"Thanks," I utter as I trudge off stage, toward the dressing room, feeling hot as hell from the lights and the conversation of choice.

Somewhere in the back of my mind, I knew this would happen.

You don't get to be out of the limelight for thirty years and pop back into public and expect no one to ask you about what you've been up to; and maybe on some level I thought it was fine, that I could handle it. Hell, I've had nightmares about this very moment.

Because I knew ten years ago, one day I *would* find my way back to the music. I just didn't know it was going to be performing alongside a sex symbol half my age who has authority issues.

When the moment *actually* came for me to take control of the narrative and tell the truth, tell my story, spin it into something positive...

I froze.

Thank God Felix jumped in.

Though I have to say, his defense, his attitude, even the small touch of his fingertips along my back was unexpected, but it felt *good.*

For the briefest few minutes, I didn't feel alone.

I felt like for the first time in years, someone got it. Got me.

I'm barely in the room for five minutes before Lou comes in, shaking his head.

"I'm so sorry, McKay. I didn't—"

"It's fine," I lie, sinking into the couch, sighing in relief as I close my eyes.

"No, it's not fine. I specifically told my guy *not* to bring up Marci, to stick to the fucking script and—"

"It's my life, and I knew by jumping back into all of this—" I wave my hand around the room, "that this was inevitable. When you're in the public eye, everything is public. Whether you want it to be or not."

Lou scrunches his eyebrows together.

"My life post *Hollow Pointe* is fine, really. Just leave Bobby out of it. That's all I ask. He's just a kid, and the last thing I want is for him to be subjected to all this Hollywood bullshit."

Lou's expression shifts as he takes a seat next to me. "You know I'd never—"

"I know," I state as a strange weight leaves me.

Lou grips my shoulder, squeezing tight. "The public's always been interested in your marriage. I thought... I thought maybe with her death behind you... you know, with it happening a good while ago, they would have forgotten about it. Hell, I thought they'd zero in on Felix and his bullshit, to tell you the truth. Kid is a magnet for attention. I guess I was wrong."

I shrug as I lean my head back in the cushions. "I mean, I married a fan. It's like, the literal Cinderella story of rock. Not to mention, I'm the only member of the band who walked away from all that shit, and I know it looks strange. Especially, given with how much Issax has remained in the spotlight. Why wouldn't they want all the details, you know?"

Lou's voice is soft, gentler as he speaks. "What do you think Marci would say about all of this?"

I sigh. "I'm sure she'd be excited because she knows how much I missed playing shows. Big ones, like this *Pillars of Rock* tour."

Lou nods. "And Felix? What do you think she'd make of him?"

I can't help but laugh. "Oh, shit. She'd probably *love* him. His pain in the ass attitude, his tattoos. Even the pink shirts. She'd probably have begged me to audition before you did."

Lou laughs. "I didn't *beg* you."

I shake my head. "No, but you clearly needed my help, and I'm not talking about the music."

Lou leans back into the cushions. The television across from us shows that Felix is on stage. I guess the show is back on the air.

"Yeah, well, you're the best brat tamer I know," Lou says with the ghost of a smile.

I know what he means, or rather *who* he means.

Isaax.

Though we've never really *talked* about those last two years, when Issax went off the rails. Before the band officially broke up.

Isaax was always insufferable, but two years into our four year run, the drugs, the alcohol, and the ever-present roller coaster of rockstar life had done a number on Issax.

I wasn't an idiot, I knew just like everyone else did that he was headed for the gutter, but like everyone else in Issax's circle, I looked the other way.

So did Lou.

But my reasons for looking the other way weren't because *Hollow Pointe* was raking in the money.

My reasons were much more personal.

I knew the moment Issax sobered up he'd forget about me, and Marci.

Forget about those hot, summer nights when

the world was at our fingertips and we were fucking immortal.

And Marci *loved* it. She loved him.

And maybe I did, too, but I wasn't going to tell him that.

Why ruin a good thing, right?

But every day I faced that truth, when I picked him up off floors covered in vomit, or pulled him from mattresses loitered with strung out, clammy bodies.

My memories slide back into those days like it was just yesterday.

Remembering the night we'd recorded *Loose Canon*. I'd performed on the track because Issax was passed out in the dressing room. That was the night Issax tried to commit suicide.

I blink furiously, trying to bury the painful memory.

Featuring me on the track was his idea. He said he didn't feel good, and he looked like shit. But then again, Issax *always* looked like shit. He was always irritable, pissy, and going off at the drop of a hat. No one wanted to argue with him.

Except me.

I wanted to run after him, but Marci and Lou told me to let it go. To record the vocals, let Issax work off whatever he needed to, however he needed to. Maybe if he got his fix, he'd relax.

I watch as Felix grips his microphone stand, recognizing the deep bass and the chime-like sound of cymbals.

The beginning lyrics of *Black Sea* in Felix's live voice are deeper, richer like velvet.

Come on in, the water's fine
Dark and tempting, it feels divine
I promise it's fine, baby, come swim with me
Don't leave me alone in the Black Sea.

His movements are short, sensual and his voice echoes with a depth, a pain that resonates on a deeper level.

I'd recorded my vocals, but something in my bones that night told me I needed to check on my bandmate.

So I did.

The doctors said if I hadn't, he would have died.

I fight back the tears from the memories as I watch Felix's fingers grip his microphone, his hair falling in his bright blue eyes.

He's not Issax, Duncan.

In my brain, I know history isn't repeating

itself. After all, Isaax is still alive and well, and still sends me a fucking Christmas card every year.

Most would think it's awkward that we don't talk much anymore, but after that night, after *Loose Canon*, everything changed.

I changed.

I saw the path my friend was on, the path I'd helped pave, and I knew I didn't want that life.

Not for him, not for me.

And certainly not for Marci.

As if he can sense my turmoil, Lou sets his hand on my shoulder. "It wasn't your fault," he says softly.

My throat constricts and I find it hard to breathe as I focus my gaze on Felix.

On his bright eyes, his glittering lip ring.

But it's not his looks that soothe my soul.

It's his voice.

Felix Heart is a complex man. His words from moments ago echo in my brain, about music, about pain.

He closes his eyes as he sings, as he digs deep into his soul, channeling the pain that he buries and laying his heart bare for the audience.

Felix is no stranger to loss, to pain.

As he sings about wanting to be a shark, but

being weak, I think about all the times I cried, all the arguments I shouldered alone.

Trying to save Issax from himself.

About all the friends I've lost to the venom of stardom.

Felix sings his haunting melodies, his raspy voice a plea for understanding, for acceptance.

That's when I realize that beneath the attitude, the alcohol, and the hotness, he's no different than me.

Trying to make sense of the world around him the only way he knows how.

Through his music.

I start to wonder, what happened to him, what or who hurt him.

Because the way he sings about drowning in the Black Sea, the haunting lyrics, and the way his entire body clutches to the microphone, the way he closes his eyes as he sings...

I have a feeling that Felix Heart has been fighting demons no one knows about, for a while.

And the drinking, the outbursts... he's just trying to quiet them, to fill the void that's been left in his heart, his soul.

I know, because I did the same thing. When *Hollow Pointe* broke up.

When Issax wouldn't return my calls.

When Marci died.

You're not alone, Felix.

"Yeah, well, I guess if you can handle Issax Perregrine, you can handle just about anyone." I say the words half-heartedly, and though my words are sarcastic, the tension in the air is thick.

Lou looks at me with silent understanding, and I know the walk down memory lane is over.

I shift my gaze back to Felix and his charged performance.

How could someone be so many different things?

An idiot, a pain in the ass, a musician, and dare I say... friend?

My thoughts wander to the way he'd stepped in when Joe asked me such personal questions.

The way his gaze lit on fire, the way his fingertips stroked my back *gently,* as if he was trying to literally soothe my nerves.

The way he'd *defended* me, on air of all things.

I couldn't remember the last time anyone jumped in to protect me, or my peace like that.

Not since my wife had been alive.

She was always tough, looking out for me and her friends. I was always content not to rock the boat, because I hated conflict, but Marci never let things go, especially if someone was being an asshole, and I get the feeling that Felix is like that, too.

He might be an asshole to most, but underneath all the bratty attitude and tattoos, he could be quite commanding.

And damn, if that isn't fucking hot.

My cheeks flush and I immediately jump up off the couch, not wanting Lou to see my sudden rush of blood. Instead, I walk closer to the TV, watching Felix belt out his heart. He opens his eyes, looking right at the camera, right at me.

I'm sure he doesn't know I'm watching him, though. He can't.

He's just channeling Felix Heart, the showstopper.

The rockstar.

But for a moment, I wish it wasn't just for show.

For a moment, I wish he'd look at me like that.

Lou gets up from his own spot on the couch, just as Felix takes his bow.

"All right then, looks like it's time for all of us to head the fuck out," he mutters, typing out a text faster than someone our age should be capable of.

"Your transport is out front. See you tomorrow morning," he grumbles as he heads out the door.

Tonight was a damn disaster.

As I decide to not wallow in regurgitated bullshit, Felix comes traipsing in, looking like he's just won the fucking lottery, but he stops the moment he sees me.

There is practically a canyon between us and I don't miss how his gaze flashes from my own, down to my groin, then back again.

He shifts his stance, giving me an ample exit, and I don't hesitate to take it.

Tonight's been too much of a curveball for me, not to mention I am tired as hell, and I know I need to get home, if only to make sure Bobby is actually sleeping and not waiting up for me.

Isn't this supposed to be the other way around?

Shouldn't I be up in bed waiting for my

sixteen year old to stumble through the door on a school night?

"You, uh... you were great out there," I say awkwardly, trying to clear the tension out of the air. My words are double edged like a sword, and I don't mean them to sound as harsh as they do.

Felix's lips twist just the slightest as he slides his hands in his pockets, taking a step forward. He nods for me to step closer, and I hate that instinctively, I do.

I take one step at a time until I am only inches away from him. Again.

How he is able to reel me in like a fish is beyond me, but I don't have the energy to fight tonight.

I'm tired, in more ways than one.

"You know, you weren't so bad yourself. All things considered."

A smile forms on my own face as I nod in response. "Thank you. For having my back out there." I say the words definitively. Truthfully, I am grateful that tonight Felix wasn't a total mess.

In fact, he was actually kind of a badass.

But I'll be damned if I admit that out loud, especially to him. He'd probably be the type to get a big head about it, parade his accomplishments around and press me for praise every chance he got, never letting me forget.

Why does the thought of *praising* Felix send a shiver through me?

Especially when it is so goddamn warm in here?

His expression softens as he smirks.

"That's my best kept secret, Duncan. I'm not actually an asshole, you know. I just play one. For the cameras."

His voice softens and sounds different.

Real.

And all at once, I understand Felix is letting his guard down.

He's letting me *in.*

And the magnitude of that is not lost on me.

"For the record, I never thought you *were* an asshole. Just a spoiled little brat," I state, my voice much deeper than I mean it to be. I mean the words to sound humorous, if only to alleviate the weird tension that has found its way back between us.

Felix chortles as he shakes his head. "Tell anyone my secret, and I'll be a lot more than a *spoiled brat* where you are concerned. I'll be a fucking *terror.*"

I can't help the smile that spreads on my face. His tone isn't malicious. Far from it.

It is playful, but also sincere, and I understand his sarcastically veiled threat.

"Noted." I nod as I take a step toward the door. "See you tomorrow, Felix."

With that, I am off, like Cinderella catching her carriage before it turns into a damn pumpkin, shedding my velvet blazer and musician visage as I enter the town car.

As I watch the city and its lights pass me by, I can't help but roll the lyrics of Black Sea around in my brain.

This is only the beginning, and I know that.

CHAPTER 14

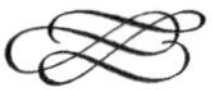

Duncan

WE'VE BEEN at rehearsal for nearly two hours, and I feel like I've run a marathon.

Maybe getting on the treadmill in preparation for this damn show wouldn't be a bad idea.

Though, of course, I'm dragging ass, too, because by the time I did get home—to find my kid sleeping like a baby, in his bed where he belonged, thank goodness—it was damn near four in the morning.

I'd barely even heard Bobby wake up, but I suppose as a parent that sixth sense will never truly leave me.

I can't remember the last time I stayed up until damn near four in the morning, passed out, and got up only two hours later and I wasn't fucked up.

Thank God for coffee and Lou's "come in at ten" text.

But Felix looks right as rain. While I practically crawled in here at nine fifty-six, Felix was already jamming away before the rest of us arrived.

How the fuck does he do that?

Especially sober?

And I can tell the man is one hundred percent, stone cold sober.

We've just finished up three quarters of the set when Lou's voice comes over the loudspeaker and he holds up my phone, which I can see through the thick soundproof glass panel.

"McKay, you've got a phone call." His voice isn't ominous, but it does impart some sense of concern, and immediately, my brain dives into the deep end of possibilities.

I barely register his words before I jump off my seat, sprinting to the door and throwing it open.

I grab the phone out of Lou's hand, pushing

past him while he barks out something at Felix and the band.

"Hello?"

My heart is in my chest as Principal Weatherby speaks on the other end.

"Mr. McKay, I'm calling about your son."

I feel like I might pass out.

"Is he okay?" I ask, my voice shaking.

"The school nurse checked him out, and he is indeed, fine, though he may have a swollen lip for a few days."

Before I can speak, he continues. "Your son had an altercation with another student in the boys locker room this morning. Several other students came forward as witnesses that he was defending himself."

My eyes fall shut in relief, and some sense of pride shoots through me.

I always told him I'd never be mad if he was defending himself. Which was why I'd insisted on boxing, but Marci won out with karate.

I guess all things considered, it still came in handy even though he quit in eighth grade.

"Oh, good," I replied, nodding even though Principal Weatherby couldn't see me.

"However, as policy states, both individuals

must be punished, all the same. We'll need you to pick your son up as soon as possible. We can discuss the terms of his suspension when you arrive."

Suspension?

For defending himself?

What the actual fuck?

Fury boils in my blood, but I know freaking out on the principal of one of the best private schools in my fucking county is probably not going to help matters. I can just hear Marci in my head, trying to calm me down.

I grit the words through my teeth, telling him I'll be there as soon as I can.

When I turn around, I see Lou and Felix both staring at me.

"Everything okay?" Lou asks gently.

Eddie and Corpse are still in the studio, tuning their guitars.

"My kid got in a fight," I say gruffly, my breathing heavy. "I have to go."

Lou nods as Felix raises his eyebrows.

"You have a kid?"

I sigh in exasperation, not in the mood to deal with Felix and his shit at the moment. I can only handle one unruly person at a time, and right now, my flesh and blood takes priority.

I push past them both, grabbing my duffel and making my way toward the elevator.

Lou mumbles something, but it is incoherent.

I press the elevator button a hundred times, anxiously awaiting the sleek silver doors to open.

Felix catches up to me, just as they open, slipping in before I can say anything.

I sigh, grinding my teeth.

"How old is... your kid?" Felix asks curiously.

"Sixteen."

"Huh." Felix's tone is careful, and I'm thankful when the elevator doors open, that I don't have to respond to him.

I slip my car keys out of my back pocket, pressing the unlock button as furiously as I banged the elevator button.

I'm tired, I'm hot, and my kid is apparently getting suspended. This is seriously the worst fucking day ever.

Felix's footsteps are still behind me, and I am annoyed.

What does he think he's doing, anyway?

Shouldn't he be inside rehearsing?

My family shit has nothing to do with him.

I'm in the car, turning the ignition within seconds, but nothing happens.

Putt putt plunk.

"Oh fuck, no, not now... not today..." I curse as I try to turn the ignition again, harder.

Putt putt putt puttttt plunk.

I try again, and again, each time to no avail. It won't kick over.

"Fuck!" I growl as the anger hits me like a volcano. I hit the steering wheel, which doesn't do shit.

My head falls against the horn, and I let out a shaky breath as a fist raps on my window.

Slowly, I turn to see Felix standing there, looking as fucking cool as a cucumber.

God damn this fucking man.

He just doesn't know when to quit.

I open the car door, raising an eyebrow at him.

"Car trouble?" he asks with a smirk that is equally annoying as it is sexy.

"What, were you a detective in a previous life?" I bite.

Felix shrugs.

"You know, I took the Porsche this morning.

I could give you a ride, if you want." His voice is even, solid and unwavering.

It's not a suggestion. It's a direct command, framed as a question.

Something about that makes me feel even more agitated.

Who is this man to tell *me* what to do?

But I also know, as I sit here, hot as hell, sweating bullets in my fucking piece of shit truck that I've had way longer than should be allowed, that I have no damn choice, not really.

I could call a taxi or an Uber, but I can never get the damn app to work, no matter how many times Bobby's shown me.

"What about rehearsal?" I say, hoping maybe he'll falter or that Lou will show up and call me a ride or...

"I mean, technically, I *am* the boss, at least where you're concerned. It's my band, so if anyone dictates shit, it's me." He shrugs apathetically. "Besides, I'm sure we could all probably use a little break. We've all been putting in the hours, not to mention you look a little beat."

Maybe because I've clearly lost my marbles.

"Fine," I utter as I get out of the car, feeling on edge. I slam the door shut, looking down at

Felix who stares up at me like he's fixing for a fight himself.

"But only because my car is having a damn meltdown at the moment. "

Felix's lips twist up in the corner, making his eyes sparkle.

"Of course." He nods for me to follow him across the parking lot to the prettiest, sleekest black Porsche I've ever seen.

I'm only partly surprised it isn't bright pink, since clearly, the man has a thing for the color.

He slides up next to the passenger door, his hands in his pockets, and I hear the clicking of the locks.

Confused, I look around, because he didn't press anything and he didn't pull out any keys.

He opens the door for me with a smile.

"It's linked to an app on my phone," he says, his tone dripping with saccharine sarcasm.

"Right." I grunt as I fold myself into the passenger seat, and he shuts the door. I watch as he pulls out his phone, tapping away a text insanely fast before he opens his own door and slips into the driver's seat.

I feel like King Kong in his sleek, fancy car, but I can't deny *he* looks good in it.

All those long limbs, tattoos, and tight pants...

I bet you could photograph him in this damn car in his everyday clothes, and he'd still sell out copies of Playgirl.

The music that blasts over the speakers makes me feel even more on the spot as the familiar sounds of *Loose Canon* ring out in the air.

"Oh fuck..." he mutters, immediately switching off. "Sorry about that." He queues up the digital screen with GPS.

I know cars nowadays have all the bells and whistles, but I've never been a fan of having computers in my car.

My truck might be one of the last cars around that doesn't even have a backup camera.

Bobby's always trying to get me to "embrace technology", but as far as I'm concerned, I don't need a computer to drive.

"Where, uh... where to?" Felix glances from me to the screen, and I realize he's waiting for *me* to put the address in.

Shit.

"Oh, uh... hold on," I reply as I lean forward, feeling oversized in the deep, ass swallowing seat.

My fingers are thicker than the keys, so it takes a couple tries to get the name of *Preston Academy* tapped out along with the address, but as soon as I do, Felix wastes no time backing out and practically speeding off.

Normally, I'd probably be concerned about how fast he's going, but with my anxious heart and Principal Weatherby's phone call, it's almost like he can't drive fast enough.

When we finally arrive at the academy, it's in record time. I'm kind of surprised we didn't get pulled over, but I'm thanking my lucky stars.

"Do you... want me to go with you?" Felix asks, and I can tell he's somewhat uncomfortable, but I appreciate his attempt to be nice.

"I'm good, thanks." I say the words much more briskly than I mean to, but I don't really have time to waste.

"I'll just stay in the car, then." He nods, chewing his lip, the lip ring jiggling from his obvious fidgeting.

I nod back and climb from the expensive seat of the car, heading into the school.

I buzz the front desk, letting them know I'm here to pick my kid up, and they let me in without a fuss.

When I round the corner to the office, I meet Bobby's gaze immediately. His eyebrows shoot up, and he looks worried, his lip swollen something fierce, streaks of dried blood accentuating the reality of what happened, but true to the Principal's word, he looks just fine otherwise.

Well, a bit shaken up, but fine physically.

"Dad!" He jumps up and I don't wait to pull him into a hug. His arms hover at my waist, as if he's afraid to return the action, but I can't say that I blame him.

I turn to see the Principal standing behind the counter. The man nods in greeting.

"We take fighting very seriously, and as such, Robert will receive a one day out of school suspension, while the other student will receive out of school suspension for the rest of the week."

I ease up a little bit knowing whatever little asshole is responsible for my kid's busted lip is at least getting some form of punishment, but I still don't think Bobby should have to be punished at all. Especially if he was defending himself.

"Understood," I say sternly as I nod at the principal.

"Come on, Bobby, let's get out of here. You

can give me the highlights on the way home." I wrap my arm around his shoulders and escort him out. Once we are out of the office, his entire body slumps and he won't even look at me.

"Bobby..."

"I don't want to talk about it, Dad, can we just..."

"No. You don't get to weasel out of this one," I say, shaking my head. "I had to leave rehearsal early, and you know I'm practically a zombie today, and—"

"Oh, I'm so sorry to be such an *inconvenience*," he bites, pushing through the solid doors.

I pick up my pace, my blood boiling once more as I chase after him.

"Don't cop an attitude with me, Robert James," I hiss as I catch up to him. I nearly knock him over as he stops, looking for the truck, obviously.

Which isn't to be found, and suddenly I feel more on the spot than ever.

"Dad, where's the—"

My heart stops as I see Felix get out of his Porsche, all languid and badass, his aviators on like he's God's gift to women and men everywhere.

The last part is a strange assumption, but I don't doubt he isn't filling some man's dreams somewhere.

Felix takes his shades off, narrowing his eyes at me and my son.

"Ah... you must be the kid," he says as he approaches us cautiously.

I don't miss Bobby's wide eyes or his stutter as he looks between us.

"Car trouble," I murmur, crossing my arms as Felix stops in front of us.

"You're—"

"Felix Hart." He nods, extending his hand and holding my son's gaze.

Bobby looks at his hand like it's made of snakes.

Though, to be fair, the snake tattoos are rather realistic looking and the dark ink covers a good bit of his forearm.

"Most people call me Bobby," he replies, politely, extending his hand carefully.

His grip on Felix is firm, which is good. I always told him you could tell a lot about a man by his handshake.

A strange sense of pride swells within me.

"Nice to meet you, Bobby." Felix nods, clearing his throat. "You hungry?" he asks, and I come back to the present.

"What?"

Felix nods for Bobby to follow him, and I'm more than shocked that my son *listens.* Without arguing.

"I know this great place, a couple minutes from here, actually, that makes the best fucking frozen yogurt, and I swear they have, like, every fucking thing you can think of to top it. Including those little juicy boba balls... Fuck, I'm getting hungry just thinking about it."

"We are not getting fucking fro-yo," I bite as Felix opens the door for Bobby, who watches me intently like a science project. As he crawls into the backseat, I head for the passenger door, but Felix beats me to it, opening it for me once more.

"No one calls it fro-yo anymore. It's just frozen yogurt." Felix rolls his eyes.

I slam the door shut, backing him up against the door as a fresh batch of anger and unfamiliar feelings swirl inside of me like a cyclone.

"He got suspended for a day, Felix. Granted,

he was just defending himself and that idiot principal—"

"My mother always said no matter what shit life deals you, ain't no one frowning when they eat a big ol' bowl of ice cream."

For the moment, his carefully constructed rockstar persona slips, and I can almost detect an actual *accent* beneath his voice, though I can't place it.

His words settle on me for a moment, and before I can protest, Felix crosses his arms and gazes up at me over his shades, pouting his studded lip as he jiggles his lip ring.

"Besides, frozen yogurt tastes a lot better than an ice pack. It should help cut the selling on his lip down, too." And with that parting shot, he opens the door for me once more, leaving me standing alone as he heads for the driver's seat.

The drive to Gustav's Gelato & More is the longest drive of my life.

"What really happened, Bobby? And don't tell me you don't want to talk about it. There is no avoiding this topic."

Bobby glares at me from the back seat.

"It doesn't matter, okay! It doesn't matter

how it started or who threw the first punch, or—"

"Did you?" Felix asks coolly. "Start it, I mean."

I snap my neck, glaring daggers at him as he speeds around the neighborhood like he owns the place.

For all I know, he just might.

Note to self to ask Lou if this pain in the ass owns any real estate out this way.

I half expect Bobby to evade Felix, but he doesn't.

He answers him without hesitation. "No, I didn't."

"But you finished it." Felix's words are not judgmental, but they are solid and direct.

It isn't a question.

"Yeah," Bobby sighed, leaning back against the cushions.

I look at him, seeing the glimmer in his eye of sadness, of pain.

Felix's lyrics reverberate in my brain once more, the ones from Black Sea, about trying to be a shark, but being weak.

Right now, I can't deny my kid looks beat in more ways than one. My heart hurts to see him like this, and anger and frustration ebb in me that there isn't anything I can do to take that pain away.

"What happened?" I ask softly.

Bobby's gaze catches mine and he frowns. "Not everything needs a reason, Dad. Sometimes people are just assholes."

Felix's voice carries through the air, the truth in his words loud and clear. "True that, Bobby. True that." Felix parks the car. He says nothing else as he gets out, heading into the shop, leaving Bobby and I alone for the moment.

Giving us space.

The notion isn't lost on me, and I have to admit, I'm surprised.

Just when I think I know Felix, he mystifies me yet again.

"I'm not mad at you, you know," I say softly.

Bobby looks at me from beneath his lashes. "I didn't think twice. He hit me, and I just... I couldn't just *let* him get away with it like everyone else does. Just because I'm..."

His words disappear, and for a moment I think he's going to tell me the truth, but instead he changes his path.

"Just because I'm different."

Something about the way he says the words feels like he means something else, but I'll be damned if I know what.

Why can't kids just say what they mean?

Why do they have to make everything so complicated?

A part of me wishes Marci was here. She'd know how to handle this situation.

I look through the windshield, through the window of the cafe. The place isn't terribly busy at this time of day, but then again, school's still in session.

It's pretty much just Felix and a couple other folks—women.

He smiles as they take selfies with him. Then he looks directly at me, and I can't help but look away.

"What happened to the truck?" Bobby asks softly.

I sigh. "Wouldn't start."

Bobby huffs as he rolls his eyes at me in disdain.

"See, if I had a car, I could just drive myself. Maybe even have picked you up." He tries to change the subject.

"If this is your way of trying to get me to buy

you a car, you need to try on a day you don't get suspended from school," I declare as I open the door.

Bobby follows, huffing his own sigh of annoyance as I head into the cafe.

My stomach growls, and I hate to admit I am kind of hungry. I didn't really eat much more than a bowl of oatmeal before heading out today.

"Grab whatever you want, it's on the house," Felix states as he hands a bowl to Bobby.

I watch as my son takes it carefully.

"Thanks," he says softly, heading toward the dispensers.

I'm about to protest when Felix whacks me in the stomach with a bowl, as well.

"You too. Maybe some *fro-yo* will change your fucking attitude, too."

"Aw, crap!" Bobby snaps as we round the corner to our street.

"What's wrong?" I ask, panic flaring once more.

Bobby closes his eyes, pursing his lips.

"I forgot, I have Study Group tonight! In, like, thirty minutes."

"What?" I ask, feeling whiplash again. "Since when did you go to study group?"

"Since the beginning of the semester... I tutor three gu— students."

Felix pulls up to our driveway, but he doesn't turn the car off.

"Where at?" Felix asks, completely unbothered by this announcement.

"Usually, we meet up at Starbucks or Percolators."

"How long is this study group?" I ask.

Bobby bites his lip. "Uh... three hours, usually. Give or take a break for food."

"It's a—"

I'm caught between grounding him indoors for the night and forbidding him from hanging out, but a part of me also knows that Bobby is more than punctual, and loyal when it comes to academics.

"You'll be home by seven," I reply sternly, and Bobby sighs.

"You need a ride?" Felix asks, but Bobby shakes his head.

"My, uh... friend... Brendan usually picks me up. He just texted me that he's almost here, so..."

Brendan... There's that name again.

I need to make a point to meet this kid. This is the second time Bobby's mentioned him, so they must be somewhat close.

Bobby's eyes meet mine, pleading with me not to make a big deal.

Felix turns the car off.

"Cool. Maybe you and I can jam out a bit while we wait for the car? Catch up on some rehearsal time?" Felix suggests, just as a little red Volkswagen shows up. Bobby immediately jumps out, looking at me.

"I promise I'll be back before dinner," he says, and I feel more than torn.

But all I can do is nod.

"Be safe and stay out of trouble." I sigh.

Bobby smiles a half-smile, but it isn't genuine. "Scout's honor."

"Was nice meeting you," Felix chirps as Bobby shuts the door, running toward the bright red bug.

I watch as it drives off, feeling more alone than ever.

There's so much I don't know.

So much I *should* know.

"My guy should be finishing up with your car. Should have it fixed and delivered before Bobby gets home tonight." Felix says, his voice cutting through the ominous silence.

I turn to look at him, to tell him no. He doesn't have to do this, any of this.

I'm tired. I'm spent.

"You don't have to—"

Felix dismisses me with a wave. "It's fine, really. It's... it's the least I can do."

Silence falls between us for a moment as he takes his aviators off, his bright blue eyes fixing their gaze on me as his expression softens.

"I assume you have a studio in there," he says softly.

I nod slowly. "Of course."

"Cool. We can jam a bit, while we wait for your truck to be delivered."

I want to argue with him, but I'm in no mood to argue, so I just say, "Okay," and open my car door.

Felix follows suit as I grab my duffel bag, fishing my house keys out of my pocket.

My blood rushes as I walk up the sidewalk, and I know it's not just from the heat.

My hands shake only a bit as I try to open the door, but thankfully, my larger frame hides me from Felix's sight.

I open the door, glancing into the entryway, and then back at Felix, who looks a bit pale.

Maybe all the *fro-yo* and the mountain of candy on top of it paralyzed him.

That weird tension is back, but thankfully, it is interrupted by Felix's phone ringing. I don't waste a moment as I head inside, leaving the door open, leaving Felix on my doorstep.

CHAPTER 15

Duncan

With the adrenaline and sugar running through me, the last thing I can focus on is music.

Not to mention, for some reason Felix being in my studio makes me nervous, so I opt to let him jam out on the couch while I busy myself with making us something to eat.

Marci always said it was impolite to have guests and not feed them, and I don't want to seem like a bad host.

Especially, given the fact that in the last twenty four hours Felix has defended me on national television, rescued me from the pitfalls of automobile hell, apparently, had my car fixed, and successfully delivered us all home in one piece without getting a fucking ticket, which is still a damn miracle.

The man must have been a race car driver in a previous life.

I watch as Felix strums away on my last project, a refurb of a Fender from '86.

The lime green color stands out against the hot pink and black, and it looks strangely fitting for him.

Maybe it's because I'm tired and this day has been hell, but I can't help the words that fall out of my mouth as I watch him play.

"It suits you," I utter, pulling his attention.

He looks up from his strumming, bright blue eyes catching mine, pouty lips opening just the slightest as he jiggles his lip ring.

"You think so?" he asks, and the question isn't sarcastic.

His fingers move over the strings lightly, black nail polish catching in the light. The sound is soothing.

I smile and nod.

"Yeah, really. You can, uh... you can keep it if

you want," I say awkwardly. "I've got a whole bunch of refurbs in my shed."

Felix smiles, nodding in agreement. "Cool, thanks."

The oven beeps and I waste no time pulling out the buffalo chicken dip.

Marci's recipe is the best and definitely is a crowd pleaser.

I set it down on the counter as Felix absent-mindedly keeps playing, though the music isn't from his set list.

In fact, it is something I've never heard before. It's softer, more melodic. Like a power ballad.

Letting the dip cool, I take my time, walking over to him.

"You've got a whole bunch in your shed?" he repeats the words as I take my seat next to him on the couch, pulling the guitar from his hands. My fingertips brush against his knuckles and he shifts his weight to make room for me, even though the couch is more than big enough to accommodate the both of us without issue.

"Started as a hobby, but kind of became more."

I angle the instrument between my legs,

strumming on it myself, trying to play the melody he just played.

I don't need to look at him to feel the heat of his gaze on me, and so, I focus on the tangible string between my fingers, and not my excited cock, or my racing heart.

I focus on the music.

"I didn't know you played guitar, too," he says dreamily. His accent slips through, and the sound is like silk.

I shrug as I strum out a few notes that I think accent his impromptu melody nicely. His thigh brushes against mine as he gets comfortable on the couch, next to me, leaning his arm against the back cushion, his head resting against his tattooed knuckles.

I steal a glance from underneath my lashes, noting his focus on me is intense.

Fuck, why is it so God damn hot in here?

I chuckle with my own sarcasm. "There's a lot of things you don't know about me, Felix."

I half expect him to bite back at me with some snippy comment about my age like he usually does, but to my surprise, he doesn't say anything bitter or sarcastic.

The faint edge of his accent slips through his words as he says, "I want to."

Something about his words exude a vulnerability, a depth that feels monumental.

I stop playing, looking up at him. His bright blue eyes glisten, the setting sun shining through the window casting shadows on the planes of his face, illuminating his bone structure.

In the golden light, in my living room, he's some perfect mix of masculine and angelic, his tongue jiggling his lip ring as he bites his lip.

"Felix..."

"I get that I'm a pain in your ass. I have been since the moment you threw me over your shoulder and tossed my ass in Lou's car." He punctuates the sentence with a laugh.

"I thought... I thought you were just some has been drummer who found God or something and just peaced the fuck out of music. Sully was always going on about how *Hollow Pointe* needed to get back together for a reunion tour, but he didn't think you'd ever agree to it."

I set the guitar down, my shoulders tightening as I prepare to defend my stance, myself.

Isaax *had* brought it up once, but at the time, Marci was going through chemo.

She begged me to accept his offer, but there was no way I was leaving her and Bobby, not then.

They were my world for so long, I forgot about the world of glitz and glamor.

Felix shifts in his spot, fidgeting, almost as if he is nervous.

But what the hell would Felix have to be nervous about?

"But the more I'm around you, it's... refreshing. I keep discovering things about you, and I want to know more. I want to know fucking *everything.*"

His voice is barely a whisper, and it is a balm to my soul.

I lean closer, capturing his gaze.

"There's not much to know, I'm afraid," I utter softly, shrugging my shoulders. "I'm not as complex as you. My life... it's simple, really. Boring."

Felix leans closer, his knee slipping into the space between my legs. Some golden hair falls in his bright eyes and he bites his lip, jiggling his lip ring again.

I'm convinced it's a nervous tick, and I have to say it's kind of endearing. It reminds me of how Marci used to bite her lip when she was being flirty.

Even spoiled, pain in the ass Felix has quirks.

"You left the business and built your own paradise, Duncan. That's not boring. It's fucking brave as hell."

My throat tightens, my heartbeat thudding so loudly in my chest I think he can hear it.

"Even paradise can be *lost*, Felix." The words are faint, almost dying in the air as I speak them.

I did have it all, but then cancer took it all away from me. From Bobby and I.

And until this moment, I hadn't really *felt* that loss.

Make no mistake, I did feel grief. Anger, pain.

But under Felix's deep blue gaze, I realize that what I miss the most is something much deeper than all of that.

Connection.

I miss that undeniable understanding, the inside jokes.

The love.

Felix leans in closer, until his face is mere inches away from mine, and somewhere in my brain I know alarm bells should be going off.

But there are none.

Not with Felix Hart.

For the first time in a long time, I feel *connected*.

I close my eyes, trying to focus on my breathing, of the magnitude of feeling running through me from this damn awful day.

Felix whispers, his breath shaky and tinged with realness that begs for acceptance. "My mama always said if something's lost, that means it can be found again."

Then I feel it.

The combination of steel and silk brushing against my lips.

A shiver runs down my spine as Felix's lips quiver against mine, almost as if he is afraid.

Consciously, I know I should push him away.

But I can't.

My entire body responds to his question as I part my own lips, grabbing him by the neck. Felix melts against me like warm butter. My tongue brushes against his piercing, and his shaky breath makes my cock twitch.

I'm overrun with feeling, with sensations

that are familiar, but that are new at the same time.

Memories flash in my brain of the woman I loved, and the man she loved.

Isaax.

I was never jealous of her feelings for him.

How could I be when I understood her attraction?

Because I felt it, too.

But I thought it was just the drugs, the alcohol.

But I know as Felix *kisses* me, both of us stone cold sober, that there is no denying I like *this*.

I'm hard as fucking marble and I can't breathe.

I'm drowning in the Black Sea, and Felix Hart is my fucking rip tide.

I can't let him pull me under.

I can't.

I push him away, fighting to give in to the overwhelming desire to grab him, to crush my lips and my fucking cock against him.

"Duncan..." His voice is soft, pleading.

I can hear the pain in it, and I know I'm about to shatter him into a million pieces.

"I can't do this, Felix," I mutter, swallowing harshly. "I—"

Felix reaches out, setting his hand on my neck, forcing me to look at him, and I can't.

Felix is wrong, I'm not brave. Not by a long shot.

I'm a fucking coward and I always have been.

"I appreciate what you've done, but I think... I think you should go."

I don't miss the glimmer of sadness, of disappointment in his gaze, and I hate it.

I hate that I'm the reason for it.

How did this get so fucking complicated?

I expect him to argue. To cop an attitude and tell me no one tells *him* what to do, but to my surprise, he doesn't fight or argue.

He drops his hand, adjusting his cock—which makes my own throb—and stands, gazing down at me.

His expression shifts, and the real Felix is replaced with someone else.

The Felix everyone else knows.

The reality of that makes me feel even worse.

"Fine. I'm sure Lex will have your car back soon enough. If there's an issue, you can call Lou."

"Felix..." I start, feeling the need to explain.

He turns his back on me as I get up, feeling like I want to chase him, but also that I need to let him go.

The truth that I don't want to let him go is like a splash of cold water and terrifies me more than I want to admit.

"See you at rehearsal, McKay."

And as I watch him leave, I curse myself and my damn cowardice.

Because I know, without a doubt, I've fucked everything up.

Apparently history can repeat itself.

CHAPTER 16

Felix

"Fucking hell!" I curse as I angrily turn my car on.

A part of me wants to wait, to see if Duncan will come running out and stop me like all those dumb movies Jinger stars in, but the other part of me—the one that wants to get as far away from the unpleasant emotions swirling inside of me—wins out.

The first thought in my brain is that I fucked up.

The second, is that I need a drink.

Or two, or three, or...

I shove the thought down, both equally pissed and unnerved that Duncan would be pissed if I went off on a bender.

Why do I give a shit what he thinks about me?

He made his feelings pretty well known when he told me to leave.

I try not to think about what happened as I drive, but it's no use.

The memory of his tongue flicking my lip ring is going to be embedded in my brain for all eternity.

"Fucking hell," I curse, but my voice isn't as angry or stern in the privacy of my own car.

It shakes because I'm weak.

Apparently, I am a sucker for drummers and unavailable men who aren't sure if they like me or not.

The highways and lights go by in a flash as I step on the gas. It's not fast enough, and the high I used to get flying around on my bike or in my fancy cars is nothing compared to what it felt like for that sliver of a moment where Duncan *grabbed* me by my neck, opened his mouth, and fucking kissed me *back*.

I arrive home in no time, and the car is barely switched off before I jump out of it.

Anxiety, anger, and worry lace through me like poison as I try to focus on breathing.

I've been in therapy enough to *know* the techniques to nip a panic attack before it gets the chance to cause a full blown meltdown, but nothing works to quell the anxiety quite like a good, stiff drink.

I find myself standing in front of my bar, frozen.

I don't even remember walking down the steps, but I'm here.

I stare at the backlit bar, stocked with everything a man could ever want or need when it comes to drinking.

But I make no move.

Instead, I stand there, staring like a dumbass as my demons taunt me.

You're not good enough for him, anyway.

How could anyone want your sorry ass?

He was married, for Christ's sake, and has a fucking kid.

He's obviously not into dick.

Except, that last one doesn't feel as truthful as the others, because last I checked, straight guys didn't get all aroused around half-naked dudes in their dressing rooms, and they certainly didn't open mouth kiss other dudes on their couches and grab their fucking necks like they *owned* them.

Fuck, now I'm hard. Again.

The bottle of vodka is calling my damn name, but so is my twitching cock, and I know it's a lesser of the two evils kind of deal.

I know I won't be able to stop at one drink. And despite the twisted and complicated feelings I have toward Duncan McKay, I can't help but think about his words to me the other day.

I need to stop treating *myself* like trash.

But that's what I am, right?

I'm not the kind of guy who grills burgers on Sunday and curls up on the couch to watch fucking Jeopardy, who tells awful punny jokes.

I'm not the man you bring home.

I'm the man you fuck on a tour bus after you've pumped your system full of X and tequila; the man you use because it's *fun* and you don't have to commit to shit.

But I want to be more than that for *someone*.

I want to be the kind of person who writes

stupid love songs, for once in my life, instead of songs about my fucking exes who I can't talk about, because God forbid anyone *knows* they suck dick.

What am I saying?

No one even knows I do, because I am no better.

The thought spirals off as I remember the feel of Duncan's arousal, pressed against me in the dressing room. It was an accident, I'm sure, but given the fact I was shirtless and in his face...

My cock throbs as images of what his dick looks like populate my brain.

I shouldn't think about such things. Really, I know I shouldn't.

Especially, given his reaction to just fucking kissing me.

The man will probably put an invisible fence between his dick and I for the rest of the foreseeable future, if he doesn't quit the band altogether because a gay asshole challenged his fucking masculinity or something.

But I can't help myself.

I slowly amble away from the bar, across the room to the couch.

When I fall into the cushions, they welcome me, and I don't wait to remove my pants, freeing my cock from its constraints.

I close my eyes, wrapping my hand around my length, and the relief is palpable as I close my eyes, stroking my cock slowly with my warm palm as I swallow harshly.

My thoughts spiral as I think about Duncan's fingers resting on my neck, of his tongue probing my lip ring, of his warm, smooth lips parting for mine.

My cock throbs and I groan. Misery laces with desire as I think about how hard I was on his couch, just from fucking *kissing* him.

I've never gotten so worked up over anyone before, like that.

I let my brain wander, filling in gaps of the fantasy like the addict I truly am.

I replay the moment over and over in my brain, the way I wished it would have gone.

His hands on my neck, and my waist, pulling me into his lap so I could feel his hardness against me, twitching, begging for me to rub against him.

"Fuck..." I hiss, as the familiar feeling builds within my stomach, my balls, my spine.

I squeeze my eyes shut, groaning as I curse, as

every nerve, every synapse fires like fireworks in the night sky, and I cry out his name when I come, feeling guiltier than ever because I know it will never happen.

I'll be lucky if he stays on the tour, period.

My abdomen spasms as I ride out the wave of my orgasm. My fingernails stroke the edge of my lorum ring as my cock throbs, emptying itself on my pink shirt.

I stare at the ceiling, feeling relieved enough for the moment, that I don't want a drink.

But what I do want, I know I can't have.

I wish I was a spoiled brat. Then, I could have everything I want.

But the truth of the matter is I'm not spoiled.

Quite the opposite, actually.

For I would give up everything just to have a shot at the kind of paradise Duncan was able to find.

A life outside of this fucking bullshit where he was *happy.*

When my cock deflates and I've sustained a sizeable puddle of cum on my shirt, I push the thoughts, the guilt, and the dreams, down into the depths of my darkness once more, locking them away.

Because if there's anything I've learned in my life, it's that I'm not meant for sunshine and fucking rainbows.

I will forever be drowning in the Black Sea and no one will ever be able to save me.

"For fuck's sake, Eddie, get your shit together," I snap, as Eddie glares at me.

"Maybe if you wouldn't rush through your songs, we'd sound better," he nips back.

I can't help that I snap at him as Duncan sighs in exasperation.

"You trying to tell me I'm the fucking problem?" I storm over to him, all but grabbing his guitar.

I haven't had a rehearsal this shitty in ages. It's like Eddie and Corpse can barely keep up with me, like they are the ones on fucking drugs.

What the hell do I know, maybe they are.

We've never exactly been the closest of bandmates. Sully was closer to them than I was, and I half expected them to follow him when he walked out on us.

On me.

Thoughts of Sully threaten to infect me again, only agitating me further.

Thanks to the rough night of sleep—two nights in a row—and the fact I haven't had a drink in days, and Duncan McKay being five feet away from me sweating like a whore in church, I'm at my wit's fucking end.

Eddie squares his shoulders. "Yeah, Felix, I am." He sneers.

I press my nose against his, my lips curling back in an angry snarl, and I want to ring his neck.

"*I* am the fucking band, asshole. *I* am the show. *I* am the reason for your fucking house in the hills. There is no *Pillars of Rock* without Felix fucking Hart!"

A crash sounds behind us as Eddie pushes me.

"Really, because last I checked you were just a pretty drunk fuckboy who won't shut up unless there's a dick in his mouth."

My fist connects with his jaw. Equipment crashes and his fist connects with my face.

I move to hit him, to hit *anything* really, as the anxiety and self-loathing kicks into gear along with years of self-preservation.

Until this moment, no one has ever said a word about my sexual preferences. It wasn't like I was open about it; but then again, I wasn't necessarily hiding it, either. At least, not from my band or Lou.

Lord knows everyone's stumbled across me with my cock down some asshole's throat, or on my knees.

It was an unspoken truth, something we didn't talk about. Just like we didn't talk about Sully's penchant for pills, or Jinger leaving his house at three in the morning.

All in the name of fame and fortune, right?

Strong arms lift me from the ground, which only makes me hurt more. Because I recognize that strength, the way in which they pick me up like I am a sack of potatoes and not a person, and I hate that I like it.

God, I am so fucked up.

I twist and turn in Duncan's arms, scrambling to try and get a hit on Eddie as Corpse holds him back, whispering something in his ear. Lou barges into the booth, his face so scarlet I think he might actually bust a vessel or have a damn heart attack.

"Enough!" he hollers.

Palo leans back in his chair, completely unbothered while Ted yawns.

I guess you've seen one band fight, you've seen 'em all.

"Corpse, take Eddie outside."

"I don't—" Eddie spits as Lou spins, glaring at him.

"Everyone take fucking five," he bites out.

Eddie breaks Corpse's hold and I finally break Duncan's.

I twist off of him, nearly falling on my ass in the process, leaving Duncan both stunned, and pissed off.

"Fuck all you, I don't need this fucking bullshit. I don't need you—" I fire as I look at Eddie, who spits at me.

"I don't need you," I hiss at Lou who looks more annoyed than anything.

"And I certainly don't need you," I growl at Duncan as I force my way past him, past Lou to the exit.

"I fucking quit," I snap as Lou calls for Duncan, his words incomprehensible to me.

Duncan grunts, his footsteps behind me an echo.

I walk fast toward the dressing room slash

lounge, wanting to get as far away from everyone as humanly possible, but it's no use.

Duncan throws open the door and slams it shut no sooner than when I make it to the corner bar.

Lou always makes sure the bar here is stocked to the brim. He knows my vices just as well as the rest of the band.

The overwhelming need for a drink is strong, but I need to be stronger.

I can't do the shit I've always done and expect different fucking results, right?

Isn't that the definition of insanity?

"What is your fucking deal today?" Duncan says. I can feel his presence behind me like an ogre. "You've been on a rip and a tear since I got here."

I stare at the clear decanter of vodka, and I swear I can smell the stringent scent like a sweet perfume.

But I can also smell Duncan's sweat, mixed with his Old Spice body wash, and guilt.

So much fucking guilt.

"Oh please, don't play innocent," I hiss, feeling the demons beneath my surface rising once more.

Memories flash in my brain of all the fights I've endured.

The men I lost because I'm not enough for them.

Because I'm an accident, a mistake.

A regret.

I can't let them hurt me.

I can't let *him* hurt me.

Duncan's eyebrows knit together, his lips pursed into a straight line, which makes the collection of coarse hair above his lips twitch, and all I can think about is how I know what it feels like, scratching against my skin.

And I'll never not know that little detail. It'll eat at me like a poison, in the dead of night, when I'm alone.

Because I'm always alone.

That's how my story ends, right?

A tortured heart writes the best songs, after all.

"Me? You're blaming your fucking temper tantrums on me? Real smooth, Felix," he growls as he angles himself closer, backing me up against the bar.

My back collides with hard metal, and the fight or flight instinct in me wants to attack.

To tell him awful things, sugarcoating my guilt and carving my desire into weapons.

The masculine scent of sweat, rock and roll, and Old Spice fills my lungs as I stare up at him with fury.

But I barely get to open my mouth, before his hand is around my throat, and like a goddamn idiot I let out a strangled sound, a cross between a groan and whisper.

My cock twitches with anticipation and I feel like I might explode into a hundred pieces. I want to fight, to argue, to tell him to fuck off.

That I never want to see him again.

But I don't get to speak.

Because Duncan presses his body against mine, his fingers tightening their grip as his fingertips brush the edge of the hair at the nape of my neck. His touch is rough, but somehow soft at the same time, scratching an itch deep within my soul. My entire body releases all its tension and I think I might dissolve into the fucking floor.

His gaze burns me, and my demons.

Words disappear as I stare up into his dark eyes, seeing my own glassy torment reflected back in his irises.

His fingers press against the throbbing vein in my neck, and the moment his lips crush mine, I snap.

His kiss is harsh, full of anger and emotions I can't quite place. I'm sure if I was a normal person, it would feel out of place, maybe even put me off.

But instead, it ignites me, somehow soothing my pain and illuminating it at the same time.

It's a blissful, rough sort of feeling and I can't help that I grab him back, my own fingernails digging into his shirt, sinking into the flesh of his hips.

His form envelopes me, crushing me like a vice, and once more I can feel his dick twitching against mine. I groan with satisfaction as Duncan nips at my bottom lip, tongue flicking my lip ring again.

I don't think anyone's ever been particularly enthralled by my piercings, and a part of me wonders if he'd give my lorum piercing the same kind of attention, which makes my cock throb against his.

The sound of his frustrated growl slash groan does nothing to quell the desire that spreads through me.

I try to catch my breath, but between his warm tongue and hard cock, I can barely think straight. I slide my hands across his hips, feeling the thickness of his form beneath me.

Duncan is a big guy.

Big, bulky, and hard as fuck.

I'm strangely into it, though.

He makes me feel smaller, lighter, and the word *prey* keeps going off in my head, dancing with other words that will probably echo in there until I write them down.

"You going to ask me to leave again?" I hiss as I trail my fingers over the outline of his length. I can feel it twitch from my touch as I grab his jean-clad erection in my hand, squeezing until he curses.

"That's not fair," he growls, his tone desperate as he grinds his cock in my hands.

I bite his bottom lip, thrusting myself against his thigh, eliciting another groan that is like music to my ears.

"No, it isn't," I bite, feeling the beginnings of precum pebbling on my cockhead.

I know in my mind, I should probably stop.

But I don't want to, and *he* isn't stopping me.

I should slow down. Ease the guy into shit.

But I don't know how to take anything slow. My entire life has been living in the fast lane.

"Fuck..." he curses, his breath shaky and his grip tight.

The truth in his voice is the final nail in my proverbial coffin.

I crush my lips against him and he presses himself into me harder, causing the bar to rock and some bottles to fall over.

"Fuck, Felix..." His voice is edged in something dark, something deep that cuts down through flesh and bone to my very being.

Underneath Duncan McKay, I feel *alive*.

Like I'm no longer drowning.

Beneath his touch, the pain subsides.

His left hand holds my hips with ferocity, his fingernails digging into my skin that is exposed through the open sides of my muscle tank, and I groan in response.

His hand slides over my hips, across my waistband, slowly until his thick fingers trace the outline of my cock, eliciting a moan that is downright desperate from my lips.

His exploration is slow and torturous, and I can't help but thrust myself against his palm, my leaking cock making a mess as I edge closer to coming, slipping my tongue in his mouth. His body stiffens for a moment, but relaxes almost instantly as he returns the action, his tongue caressing mine.

Fucking prey, indeed.

The sound of the door opening is like a damn bucket of ice water, and I barely have time to process the moment.

Then again, I don't think I could process *anything* with Duncan all over me, touching me, kissing me. Bringing me to the edge of salvation.

For the first time in my life, I feel a sense of worry.

Not because I don't want to be found with Duncan, like *this,* but because somewhere in my feeble brain I know that this is unfamiliar territory for Duncan.

Hell, I am probably the first guy he's ever kissed, and that alone is probably throwing him a fucking curveball, and now...

Duncan moves away as Lou coughs, and I'm painfully aware of my rigid erection and the wet spot forming against my damn underwear.

Jesus Christ.

Duncan doesn't look at me, but he doesn't have to.

I can feel the panic, the anxiety, like it's a person all on its own.

Lou opens his mouth, and I watch as Duncan's shoulders tighten, those broad muscles thick and tight.

Fuck that is *not* helping my current situation.

"It's not what it looks like," Duncan bites out, and though I'm not surprised at the reaction, I am still hurt.

I can't think rationally with my cock throbbing in my pants.

Lou looks between us, and I do nothing to hide the evidence.

Lou's seen a lot worse.

"I was going to say it looks like everything is under control here," Lou announces smoothly, settling his gaze on Duncan. "Eddie is calmed down, and wants to apologize." Lou doesn't look at me.

"Good, he was being a dick," I utter as I adjust my erection.

"Duncan, can you give Felix and I a minute alone, please?" Lou flashes me a glare.

Fuck.

"Yeah, of course." Duncan grunts as he ambles through the space, heading for the door. When he shuts it, the temperature drops in the room.

"I don't know what game you think you're playing, Felix, but you need to be careful," Lou warns, his voice edged in darkness, filled with a concern I've never heard before.

His gaze makes me feel small, but not in a good way.

Definitely not how Duncan makes me feel.

"I'm not playing a game, Lou." It's the truth, but I don't know if he buys it.

"You know I've never had a problem with your... preferences. What you do with your dick is your business, as long as—"

"As long as I keep it out of the public eye, I know," I bite. "God forbid anyone knows Felix Hart is gay. The world will fucking end."

Lou purses his lips, his gaze dark and serious.

"You are playing with fire, Felix."

I cross my arms, meeting his solid gaze. "Maybe I like getting burned," I snap.

Lou shakes his head. "It's not *you* I'm worried about."

The gravity of his words hit me, and suddenly, I feel like a gigantic asshole.

Which is fitting, because I *am* a giant asshole.

"Not everyone can withstand a fire, Felix. Some people have already been burned enough."

With that, he turns on his heel and strolls from the room, leaving the door open.

CHAPTER 17

DUNCAN

IF ANYONE TRIES to tell you banging on drums is *not* a form of therapy, they are lying.

Because honestly, it's what's saving me from completely walking out this door.

My entire body is still racing from adrenaline.

From kissing Felix.

Though, I know when Lou walked in on us, I was headed toward a lot more than just kissing.

What was I thinking?

You weren't thinking with a clear head, that's for sure. Not with the right head, anyway.

Eddie did apologize to Felix, but the tension between them could still be felt in the air, which didn't help matters.

When we wrap the last song, I pack up my shit without a second thought and bolt out of the studio.

True to his word, Felix's guy did drop off my car last night, not long after he left, and I have a feeling he did a hell of a lot more to my car than just fix the starter.

For God's sake, the inside *smelled* like brand new car, but I was certain it wasn't a new car.

I checked the backseat, where Bobby painted his initials in the door plastic with his mother's nail polish. Nothing took that shit out, and it was still there.

I offered to pay the guy, but he'd only told me, "it was taken care of," which made me feel awkward as hell, so I made sure to at least give the guy a hefty tip and told him I wouldn't take no for an answer.

A part of me, the insane part who is probably responsible for kissing Felix instead of telling him off, wishes he'd come running out of the studio to stop me from leaving.

To tell me we never have to talk about what happened again.

That we can just go on with our lives like nothing happened.

But I know as I get into my driver's seat, turning the ignition, which *purrs* now instead of hisses, that that is just not going to happen.

There is no way in Hell I am ever going to be able to forget Felix buckling underneath my grip, or his throaty fucking moan when I touched him, or how my entire body vibrated at the sound.

"Fuck!" I hiss as I back out of the parking lot, speeding onto the highway.

The last thing I want to think about right now is Felix and his deep blue eyes, his pouty lips with that goddamn lip ring, and his fucking *attitude*.

When I auditioned for this gig, I thought I knew who Felix was. I thought he was just some spoiled rotten rockstar who got too famous too early, who was just a pain in the ass who needed someone to put him in his place.

Make no mistake, he is still a pain in the ass who needs someone to put him in his place, but the reality that I *want* to put him in his place—in a way that is more than highly unprofessional—only makes this whole situation worse.

For starters, I'm straight. I have been my whole life. Never have I *ever* had *feelings* for another man.

Attraction?

Maybe?

I'm not sure what Issax and I had could be classified as anything other than circumstantial. Yes, I loved the guy, but not like I loved my wife.

We were brothers in arms, not... boyfriends.

It was the damn eighties, man. We were all fucked up six ways from Sunday most of the time, and my wife likened to the filling in a *Hollow Pointe* sandwich. So sue me if I *liked* it, too.

Though I'm not entirely sure how much of that was me and how much was a desire to please my wife, and how much was because I was wasted and young.

It was just part of who we were.

I grip the steering wheel tighter as I grind my jaw.

Second, Felix is half my age. Christ, he's closer to Bobby's age than he is mine.

Third, I might've had my fair share of Issax

and Marci, but prior to being in the band, I hadn't really had *that* much experience with women, but I knew I liked pussy.

That has to count for something, right?

I groan as I count down all the reasons I should fucking put an end to this damn gig.

I turn up the radio, needing to focus on something else, because all I'm doing is thinking in circles, and every path cycles back to Felix Hart.

And because God has an awful sense of irony and humor, the first song I hear over the radio is *Carnage.*

You think you can escape the devastation you leave in your wake.

But you can't fight the carnage, baby, because your carnage is mine to take.

God, it's like I can't get away from the guy.

But do I want to get away from him?

Or do I want him to ruin me?

When I finally make it home, much later than I planned, thanks to some construction hold up, I walk in the door and am immediately accosted with the smell of sweet, smokey barbecue and aromatic cheese.

My stomach growls at the scent and I see my son flitting about the kitchen.

He looks up to see me as I close the door.

"What's all this?" I ask, knowing I *should* still be somewhat pissed at him for getting suspended for a day, but finding it very hard to be mad when he's making dinner that smells better than any five star restaurant.

He knows just how to play his cards.

Smart kid.

"Dinner," he says softly, his gaze dancing with slight alarm.

Before I can ask what's wrong, or what he wants—because this dinner smells like he wants something—he opens his mouth.

"There's... something I need to tell you. But first, let's sit down, okay?"

The tone of his voice is uneven, and I can tell he's nervous, which, on top of my already frayed nerves, makes my adrenaline spike again.

But all I can say is, "Okay," gruffly as he fixes a plate and hands it to me.

I sit down, letting the potent scent of melty cheese and sticky barbecue pork soothe my soul, if only for a brief moment.

Bobby sits across from me with his fork poised in his hand, and my stomach flips.

I don't know how much more shit I can take today.

I grab my fork and stab a macaroni noodle.

"So... what's got you all Martha Stewart in the kitchen today? What are you buttering me up for?"

Bobby takes a bite of his barbecued brisket before looking me dead in the eyes.

"Yesterday, I got into a fight with another student because..."

I set my fork down, noting the pain that comes over his face.

But he steels his resolve, swallowing it down like a macaroni noodle.

"Because Callahan called me, and I quote, 'a piece of shit cock chaser bottom who could only get into college if I fucked my way onto the dean's list.'"

My blood boils, and my immediate thought is I want to *murder* this kid.

What kind of kid thinks they can go around saying that kind of shit to another person?

Bobby's smarter than most of those kids in

that pricey ass school. For God's sake, he's been in gifted since he was in the fourth grade.

"I told him to fuck off and leave me alone… maybe with some choice words about how he's failing everything but gym and the only way he was going to get in anywhere was is if he could actually score a touchdown, and… and then he got in my face and called me a fag, and then he insulted Brendan, and… and then he hit me, and —" His words come out almost all at once without a breath in between.

I set my fork down as I watch Bobby's face fall.

There's that name again, Brendan.

"I just, I didn't want to be another victim, Dad. I wanted to show that asshole that just because I'm…"

The silence between us is palpable, and I think for a moment he's going to evade me again.

But he doesn't.

He looks right at me, his eyes glassy as he says two words that ultimately change everything.

"I'm gay."

There's a lot of things you hope you never hear as a parent. Whatever it was I thought he was going to say didn't matter. Not now.

I thought he was in trouble. That he was going to tell me he knocked up some girl or that he'd gotten caught doing something he shouldn't have. I know he's a good kid, but these last few years he's been so isolated, so quiet, I wasn't sure he *wasn't* going through something monumental, but all the parenting blogs advocated I not push the issue, so I didn't.

But never in a million years did I ever think I'd hear those words come out my kid's mouth.

I'm gay.

I know my response is pivotal, and will forever change the course of our relationship.

I look at him, underneath the dining room chandelier lights, at his soft green eyes and perfectly windswept hair, and I see myself, but I also see the sparkle of Marci shining through in his bravery.

Because without a doubt, coming out to me like this, in general, takes fucking balls.

There's a hundred things I could say, but all I settle on is, "Oh."

Bobby raises an eyebrow. "Oh? Really? I tell you this big thing, and all you can say is *oh?*"

"Can I ask you a question?" I pick up my fork.

Bobby blinks, looking a little worried. "I mean, sure, I guess."

"How long have you known?" I ask delicately. "That you're gay, I mean."

Bobby shifts in his chair, pursing his lips as he stabs at some pork. "Since I was fourteen. I guess."

Two years.

The realization makes me feel like somehow I've failed.

As a parent, as a person.

"How do you... *know*?" I ask, not meaning to sound harsh, but not able to hide the pain and disappointment that he kept something like this from me for so long.

I'm not sure what I would have done, or said, but it's my job to *help* guide him. To make sure he's safe, and happy, and—

Bobby shrugs, catching my gaze. "I mean, how do you know you're straight?"

His words make my throat constrict, my blood run cold.

Because they sound like an accusation, and despite my desire to answer him and tell him 'I just know', I don't.

Because the moment he says those words, all I can think about is Felix.

I'd told him to leave last night, not because I didn't *like* what was happening, or because I felt uncomfortable, but...

Because I *did*.

I did like the feel of his lips, the metallic taste of his metal in my mouth, the little groans and whimpers that escaped his throat.

I did like how pretty he looked playing my guitar, lit up by the sunlight in my house.

Shit.

Does that mean I'm *not* straight?

I swallow harshly and my stomach flips, and I blink as I try to process this information.

"I, uh... guess that's a fair point," I say evenly, despite my insides feeling like a building has collapsed and we're short on first responders.

"You're not... mad?" he asks in the smallest voice, and I hate that he expects such behavior from me.

He's my fucking kid.

My flesh and blood.

How could I be mad at him over something like *this*?

"I'm not mad at you, Bobby. Not about you being gay. I'm a little pissed you got in a fight and got yourself suspended for a day… Even though I am equally proud you gave that asshole what he deserved, your mother would tell you violence isn't the answer to anything, and she would be right."

Bobby raises one eyebrow. "Did you say you're *proud* I hit that kid?"

I can't hide the half-smile on my lips as I nod in response. "Yes, I did."

His half smile melts my heart just a fraction, as I continue.

"However, I am a little disappointed you didn't come to me sooner. Two years is a long time to keep a secret. That can't have been easy. You must have felt so alone…"

I can only imagine.

He frowns as he pushes around his macaroni. "I wanted to t tell you, but—"

"But what?" I ask.

"I guess I just needed time to figure some stuff out on my own first."

This entire conversation is uncomfortable, but parenting in general is uncomfortable.

Doing it alone is like scaling a mountain. It

just gets harder the further up you go. But that doesn't mean it's not worth it.

"So this Callahan, he knows you're gay? Are you two—"

"Oh God, no!" Bobby says adamantly. "He's so not my type. He's an asshole for one, and two, he's not even that good looking, and three, he's not even *that* good an athlete, and four—"

I hold my hand up. "I get it. Maybe he likes... you?" I suggest, thinking about all the boys I'd known growing up, before I signed with the record company.

It wasn't an uncommon behavior for guys to be total dicks to the girls they liked, because they liked them.

Maybe it worked the same way for guys who liked guys?

As I ask the question, my mind filters in thoughts of Felix and his downright bratty attitude.

Is that what was happening between *us*?

Is... Felix gay?

Or is he like me?

He's been tied to a lot of women in the press, but I know how the rumor mill and tabloids worked. It didn't mean any of it was true...

Isaax never shied away from his sexual image, but he wasn't exactly talking about our group sex antics. The world would have lost their minds, and I wasn't too keen on the world knowing what I did behind closed doors with my wife.

God, I am so out of my element here.

A strange thought permeates my brain and I wonder if sexual preference is hereditary.

It's not, right?

Bobby rolls his eyes. "No, he's just an asshole who thinks he can catch the gay." His voice is sarcastic, but somehow humorous. "Like Felix said, some guys are just assholes."

I shrug as I take a bite of my macaroni, which has finally cooled down enough it won't burn my tongue.

"You know, for the record, guys are dicks. Seriously."

Bobby laughs. "Yeah, but some aren't. Some are just hard on the outside, and squishy on the inside. Some are worth a hundred Callahans."

Something about his words soothes something in my soul.

Sometimes kids can be wise beyond their years and not know it.

Sometimes, they can heal you, too.

My next words are careful. I can appreciate the delicacy of the situation, and I know right now I'm not fucking things up, so I'd like to keep it that way. Keep the channel open for my son to come to me if he needs to, even if it makes me uncomfortable because I don't know probably half of what he does.

"Is it safe to assume you, uh... have someone in your life who is worth a hundred Callahans, or..."

Bobby blushes, and I know without his admission the answer is yes.

"Um... I mean... not really... but... sort of."

I take a bite of a mouthful of noodles. My God, if this kid doesn't end up in a culinary career, he will make one hell of a husband.

"Sort of? Last I checked relationships were pretty much you're either in or you're not."

Again Felix's words filter through my brain, along with the memory of his fingers grabbing my hips.

I shove the thought away.

"Unless...." I twist my lips. "This person doesn't *know* you like them."

Bobby sighs, as he takes another bite of his dinner.

"It's complicated."

"For the record, if you can punch that asshole Callahan and come out to me over a plate of the best mac and cheese I've ever had, I'm pretty sure you can handle anything."

Bobby smiles. "Thanks, Dad."

I nod in response as we eat the rest of our dinner.

AFTER CLEANING up and making sure I'm giving my kid enough space, I retire to my studio cave.

Though, I was able to channel my best face for my kid and focus on him and his needs—which included a hug and a reminder that our home is the safest place for him to be *honest* with himself and with me—I knew, eventually, I'd have to deal with my own dishonesty.

I couldn't help but think about Bobby's words when I'd asked how he knew he was gay.

I asked, because I was curious how he'd come to this determination on his own, not because I didn't believe him.

But as I asked the question, and as he

answered, 'How do you know you're straight?' I found myself feeling like the world had just exploded in front of my very eyes.

Because I couldn't say with one hundred percent certainly that I am straight.

But I couldn't remember ever *wanting* Issax to touch me the way Felix did.

After Issax went to rehab, Marci and I both decided to put an end to bringing anyone else into our lives. We wanted to give the white picket fence thing a real shot.

Then Marci got pregnant, and suddenly, nothing else really mattered.

All we needed was each other, and our kid. She was happy. I was happy.

After she died, I couldn't fathom wanting anyone else. Not even Issax.

The hole she left was far too big for anyone to fill, and I had a six year old to take care of.

I couldn't afford to be selfish, and I didn't think finding another wife was the answer, no matter how many people told me I needed to find Bobby a "new mom."

As if anyone could replace the perfect one who gave birth to him and raised him.

Of course, I was lonely, but I wasn't *alone.* I

had family, friends from the neighborhood. I had Bobby.

As far as I was concerned, I didn't need to date anyone, and sex...

Sure, I missed it, but I couldn't picture myself sinking my cock into another woman who wasn't my wife. I still can't.

But the moment Felix *touched* me, squeezing my damn cock in the studio dressing room...

I close the door, falling into my chair, swiveling back and forth as that question ricochets in my brain.

How do you know?

I look at my computer screen, thinking about the last time I was in the room, looking up articles on Felix.

Looking at his full nude spread in Playgirl.

Him all slathered up in oil, showing off more than just his lip ring.

My cock throbs at the thought, and an idea forms in my brain.

As a kid, I wasn't a stranger to going through my dad's Playboys, but as a teenager, I didn't *need* to look at tits or ass in a magazine when it was practically thrown in my lap every day.

Which is how I met Marci to begin with.

When she cornered me on the *Hollow Pointe* tour bus after a show in Pasadena.

I type in "threesome" into Google, figuring that's at least a good place to start, right?

A list of search results comes up, from YouTube videos to Cosmopolitan articles telling you how to practice safe throuple sex.

Throuple?

There's a *word* for it?

I almost shut down the search, thinking I am clearly out of my league. Until I stumble upon a result that reads MMF threesome.

I don't think twice about clicking it.

The video that fills my screen is one I can't look away from.

A curvy woman with bright red hair is being pinned against the wall while a much larger man spears her, his fingers digging into her sides as he rails her, making her rather large breasts jiggle from each pounding.

It's hot, I won't deny that, but my gaze is fixed on the man behind *him.*

The tall, thin, and certainly less muscular man that walks in, who I guess is supposed to be the husband or the boyfriend, home from work early who finds his wife being porked by the service man.

A typical plot, I guess, if you're a frequent porn watcher.

Which I'm certainly *not.*

But I can't tear my eyes away as I watch the tall blond's graceful movements, the way he slinks across the room, undressing as he goes.

Once his clothes are off, we get an ample money shot.

The guy is hung like a damn horse, and my cock twitches at the sight. I'm transfixed on the way he slides his hand over his rigid rod, approaching the man, who ignores him, continuing to pound away at the woman beneath him, making her thighs jiggle as much as her breasts, which he adamantly starts sucking on.

I can't help but slide my own hand in my pants, my own hardness twitching from the touch. I slowly stroke myself as I watch the tall blond tease the other man with the head of his cock, telling him to keep going.

I watch as the other man arches his back, biting out some sort of incoherent mumble, in which, the blonde retaliates.

He *spits* on his cock and my own throbs as I build my rhythm.

I settle in on an even pace, keeping in time with the thrusts of the men on screen, but it feels lackluster.

I keep stroking, squeezing, but I'm no closer to coming, even when it's clear that everyone has reached their pinnacle.

My head falls back against the cushion of my chair as I huff out an annoyed grunt.

I knew this was a bad idea. I should just let it go, go to bed and forget about this stupid little experiment.

But I also know I'm halfway there, and I hate to go to bed with the guilt and shame that comes with *not* getting off.

Even if it is in the privacy of my own home.

I sit up, noticing the video log has queued up some other results. Since I'm already committed to my dick, I figure clicking on something else is probably the best option.

Before I can make a decision, another video starts playing, so I figure the autoplay will roll into something similar. Another MMF video, perhaps.

But I soon discover this video is *not* a threesome.

It's a twosome, between two men, and I cannot tear my eyes away.

One is a larger guy, and pretty hairy, while the other is as smooth as porcelain.

My cock twitches as I watch the tall, pale, lanky man drop to his knees. The camera pans to show a close up of his face, the larger man's swollen cock in full view.

Holy fuck, he's *thick.*

The look on the lanky man's face is almost like he's been drugged. It's euphoric as he opens his mouth, pushing his tongue against the slit of the cock before him. Groaning and licking until he opens his mouth, swallowing down the monstrosity before him.

I watch as thick hands slide through his disheveled dark hair, as his mouth endures a good, hard fuck that makes his damn eyes water, and I groan as I feel my own cock pebbling with moisture.

I close my eyes, letting the sounds fill my cave.

I imagine pouty lips and cold steel against my leaking slit, familiar groans and bratty grunts accentuating the sounds from my entertainment.

It's too much.

I open my eyes, watching as the larger man's cock disappears down the other man's throat again, and I know there is no denying I like this.

The realization hits me just as I come to that edge, as the door opens and everything goes to hell.

"Oh my God!" Bobby hollers as he turns around.

"Fuck!" I hiss, sitting up in my chair, with the worst blue balls of my life.

If there is ever anything to kill the mood, it's having your kid walk in on you in the middle of masturbating.

To gay porn.

Fuck!

"Jesus Christ, Bobby, don't you know how to knock?" I hiss as I hurry to shut off the moans and sounds coming from my computer screen.

"I did. You didn't answer, and I got worried... I thought maybe you fell asleep at the computer, or—"

I lean forward, running my hand over my face, and I can't help but bust out laughing.

"What's so funny?" Bobby mutters.

I shake my head. "I'm just thinking how this should be the other way around," I reply as he turns, his cheeks still red, but he glances at me, his eyes questioning. "I'm supposed to be the one to walk in on you."

"This isn't because of what I said... is it?" I can see the panic in his eyes. "Because if you have questions, you can just ask me... I'll do my best to give you better resources than..." He glances at my computer, raising an eyebrow. "Pornhub? Seriously, Dad..."

I sigh, as the words tumble out of my mouth without warning, clearly because I've lost my marbles. "I needed to know... for myself."

Bobby's eyes widen as his mouth falls open. He blinks like I've been replaced by an alien.

And I'm sure, to him, this is news is huge.

Hell, it is for me, too, and I'm the one who just got caught with my hand in my pants.

"Oh." He nods, his blush still coloring his otherwise pale cheeks.

"Oh? That's all you can say?" I quip, laughing like an idiot.

Bobby laughs, too, all of a sudden, and for a moment, all that can be heard is our hysterics.

When we finally catch our breath, I ask, "What did you want? Before you so rudely interrupted me." I clear my throat.

Bobby shrugs. "I wanted to ask you if I could bring a friend over... tomorrow. For study group."

I nod. "You don't have to ask me permission. I appreciate you doing so, but it's fine."

"I mean, you're not like... grounding me or anything because of what happened, right?" He leans against the doorway.

I shake my head. "No. But if I get another call about you hitting someone or getting in a fight, you will be."

Bobby smiles and says, "Okay," as he turns toward the hall, when he stops, turning to look at me once more. "Hey, Dad?"

"Yeah, kid?"

"I love you. No matter what. I just... wanted you to know that."

My heart feels like it might burst out of my chest as my throat constricts again.

"Ditto, Bobby."

CHAPTER 18

FELIX

I'VE BEEN to the Sylverstro's mansion a dozen times, and honestly, I'm not all that impressed.

You've seen one compound, you've seen them all.

The California air is hot, unseasonably warm for this time of day, or more accurately, night, since the sun will be setting in about an hour. Which is why most of us have taken to corral together inside the house, instead of on the extensive verandas.

I watch as waitresses parade on by with their trays of champagne, feeling utterly bored.

I've never been a fan of label events. Which is why I'm usually fucked up beyond all repair before the sun goes down.

Where the hell is Duncan?

Since our moment the other day, he's barely said two words to me.

I'm trying my best to be patient, to wait it out and see what his next move is.

My anxiety keeps building, thinking he's going to just leave, like Sully, and then I really will have an issue, being as the So-Fi show is a little more than a week away.

"There's my favorite fucker." A voice pulls me from my thoughts, and I immediately tense.

My gaze falls on Dare Wylde, the lead guitarist and singer from *Heart Killer*.

I don't *dislike* the guy, but he's annoying as fuck.

Small doses, that one.

"Dare," I murmur, as he makes his way over to me, two drinks in hand. From the look of the grin on his face, I'd surmise he's at least five or six in, at this point, and that makes me feel even more out of place.

He offers one crystal glass to me. "You look like you need a drink."

I almost tell him no. But as I look around at everyone else, all schmoozing it up for press for this damn kickoff tour, I cave.

I grab the glass, my fingers brushing against his tattooed knuckles. I take a sip. It's some fruity shit that is most certainly *not* vodka, that someone like Dare should be embarrassed to be drinking in public, but it isn't terrible. It's likely ninety percent sugar, so I suppose it's better than nothing.

"Thanks," I murmur, licking my lips.

"What's your problem tonight, sourpuss?" He laughs, his vibrant red contacts catching the light. He runs a free hand through his jet black gelled hair, shaking his head a bit.

"Excuse you?"

"You've been in the fucking corner, watching the damn door since you got here. Either you're waiting for a supplier—" He licks his lips, grinning at me.

Of course, that's why he's here. He wants drugs.

"Nope. Not my cup of tea anymore. That's Sully's department."

Dare raises his eyebrows. "You going cold turkey clean, Hart?"

The surprise in his voice makes me loathe

myself even more. Because the way he says it, is the same way a kid says "Santa's not real?" Like they don't fucking believe it.

I take a long pull of my sugary punch disguised as an actual drink, and shrug.

"Maybe, I just want to stop feeling like fucking trash when I wake up."

Maybe, I just want more.

Is that so fucking crazy?

Dare shakes his head as he drains his drink. "I ain't judging you, man. You do what you gots to do,." he slurs.

Something about his words makes me feel like he's hiding something, but what, I can't tell.

"Oh my God, Lixxxy!" Jinger singsongs and I roll my eyes.

Dare laughs, passing his drink off to a waitress as Jinger saunters over to us, dragging Geo Graves, the lead singer of *Gravedigger* with her. His black shirt is popped open, displaying his giant medieval cross tattoo that spans his entire chest and abdomen.

I've lost track of how many tats I've acquired, being as half of them were acquired when I was drunk, but Geo's got to be the only one on the label with *one* tattoo.

Even Jinger has, like, four. All strategically placed, of course, to heighten her sex appeal.

Like butterflies are considered sexy.

Whoever came up with that idea is an idiot.

"I've been looking for you all evening," she coos as she abandons Geo, throwing her arms around me, rocking me and making my drink slosh.

I peel her off of me as Dare and Geo chuckle.

"Yes, well, I can't return the sentiment," I mutter as she pouts.

"You're such a killjoy," she mewls, crossing her arms.

"I don't know about you guys, but I am so ready for this fucking show next week." Geo groans, rubbing his neck.

Dare shrugs. "Ready for the flashing lights and the screaming fans."

Geo chuckles. "The only screaming is going to be for you to get off stage," he razzes Dare.

"Fuck you, asshole," Dare slurs, swaying backward a little.

Jinger giggles as Geo gives the finger to Dare. I roll my eyes.

I know we're all a mix of ages, but I swear these guys act like damn teenagers.

As I break my gaze from the riveting discussion in front of me, I turn to see Duncan on the other side of the room.

His gaze catches mine, and my heart skips a beat.

Clearly, he's utilizing the capsule collection I sent him. His deep, gold silk shirt is unbuttoned at the top two buttons, his leather jacket accentuating the ochre tones perfectly. Combined with the fitted black jeans and boots, he looks more like the Duncan from *Hollow Pointe*, than the Duncan in faded jeans and vintage tanks.

His deep brown eyes pull me in like a fish on a damn hook.

"If you'll excuse me, I'm going to extricate myself from this riveting conversation," I state, as Jinger laughs, Dare questioning what the fuck *extricate* means.

I make my way across the foyer, until I meet Duncan on the other side.

"I wasn't sure you were going to show up," I say gruffly.

Duncan slides his hands in his pockets, cocking his head to the side, his thick, neatly trimmed eyebrows furrowing.

My gaze dips to his trimmed beard, to his

mouth where he's sporting the slimmest sliver of silver.

A fucking lip ring.

My cock throbs at the sight as thoughts fill my brain of what that would feel like against my thighs, scratchy beard and cool metal.

What it would feel like pressed against the slit of my weeping cock.

Fuuuuck.

I swallow hardly, trying not think sexy thoughts.

But I find that's extremely difficult when I am ninety percent sober and in the presence of this mountain of a man.

"Lou said it was mandatory press for the tour, so..."

"Right." I nod as both relief and disappointment flood me. Relief because he's acknowledging the tour, which means he must be staying, but disappointment because maybe he *doesn't* want to be here.

And because I'm a goddamn glutton for punishment, I quip, "You clean up nice."

Duncan cracks a half smile, but it's genuine and warms my insides better than any fruity concoction.

Which I take a sip of, if only to keep myself from spewing more stupidity.

"Yeah, well. It helps when someone else picks out my clothes. If it were up to me, I'd be in a Slayer shirt and a pair of blue jeans."

I smirk at him. "Honestly, it might be this..." I tap my own lip ring. "Really pulls the whole outfit together."

Duncan slides his hands in his pockets, slowly walking us around the round foyer.

"I thought it wouldn't be a bad idea to revive the look. For the tour, anyway."

I take the lead. "Let me give you the unofficial tour, of the Sylvestro's palace," I offer before I start spouting sonnets about his perfect, pierced mouth.

After one drink, that should be a record. I pawn off my empty glass to a waitress passing by, waving about to the first room.

"That over there is the kitchen, full of fancy schmancy shit that tastes like fuckin' cardboard, then you've got the great room, where all the corporate assholes hang out." I wave at the great room. I catch Lou in my sight, who sees us, and Duncan waves.

Lou doesn't get up, but he nods at us as I continue my tour.

"This is the living room, or one of the four living rooms, technically, where all the producers hang," I say, pointing out Palo and the other studio producers.

I gesture to the area of the room I occupied previously, pointing out Geo, Dare, and Jinger. The only one missing from the bunch is *Mage Of Mercy*'s lead singer, Mateo Starr, aka Matty, but he's always been reclusive, even for a rockstar of his caliber.

I wouldn't be surprised if he's holed off somewhere on one of the top floors, where no one else is, just so he can avoid the rest of us.

"And what about up there?" Duncan points to the grand staircase, to the balcony that over-looks everything.

"Four bathrooms, a game room, and of course, guest bedrooms. Third floor has the master, plus a conservatory, and a music studio. That's probably where Mateo is."

I watch as Duncan slides his hand up the staircase banister, my gaze falling on his perfect, round ass as he slowly ascends the stairs.

He turns his head to look at me over his shoulder, raising an eyebrow. "Well, are you coming or what?"

I sigh, knowing I'm sealing my doom.

Of course, I will go wherever this man wants me to go. I'd rather be around him than Jinger and Dare.

Geo's okay... but his straight edge former Christian rock shit gets on my nerves. The guy is about as pure as Colombian cocaine, despite his aesthetic.

I skip ahead of him, if only so I can illustrate dramatically the beauty of the main feature of this damn staircase.

The gigantic crystal chandelier.

"And of course, we can't miss the *Phantom Of The Opera*," I say sarcastically as Duncan looks up. I find a spot on the landing, over the railing, watching as Duncan slowly makes his way upward, his eyes as wide as saucers.

"We didn't do press anywhere like this, in my day," he states absentmindedly.

"Yeah, well, in your day, I'm sure you walked barefoot uphill in the snow both ways to the radio station."

Duncan shoots me a glare, and I bite my lip.

Sometimes I wish I had a filter.

But alas, if I thought about everything before I said it, I wouldn't have four Grammy's.

That's the beauty of being a singer slash songwriter. Sometimes, the lack of filter is best when it comes to writing songs.

Duncan makes his way over to where I stand, and suddenly, I feel hot. This close, I can smell his heavenly Old Spice scent mixed with cologne, and it makes my mouth water. Combined with his gold shirt and the sparse gray and brown chest hairs poking through his collar opening, I can't deny I am attracted to the man.

Why do I always want what I can't fucking have?

His expression changes, hardening, and a tension breeds between us.

"Is there somewhere we can... talk?" he inquires, swallowing harshly.

Panic floods me as he adds, "Privately, I mean? You know, before the press junket. Get some things, uh... straight?"

My heart sinks at his words. Get things *straight*.

Like, where we fucking stand before the cameras start flashing.

I nod toward one of the rooms on the other end of the hall, the opposite side of where the press is starting to gather. It usually takes a bit for them to trickle in, which is why we all arrive so bloody early.

"Yeah, of course," I reply as nonchalantly as possible, trying not to betray the fact I feel like I'm walking to my doom.

Maybe he's *not* staying. Maybe this is why he came. To tell me he's leaving.

Just like Sully.

Just like every other man in my damn life.

I lead us into the room, opening my mouth to ask him what's up, but I don't get the words out.

Because the moment the door slams shut, my back is pressed against it, and Duncan's lips are on mine, his hand settling at my throat, squeezing with the lightest of pressure, but warm to the touch.

The moment he kisses me, I melt into him like a fucking puddle in a damn swoony rom-com.

His metal clashes with mine as our tongues dance together.

When he breaks away, his amber gaze is full of fire, his lips glisten, swollen from our kiss.

A hundred emotions fester beneath my boiling surface, from excitement to happiness, to anger and anxiety.

Because as much as I want to continue this shadowy makeout, I also want more, and the feeling is as shocking as it is new.

For the last seven years, I've taken whatever I could get, wherever I could get it.

I've never once felt like I *deserved* more than what I'd had.

But as I look at Duncan McKay, feel his body pressed against mine, hand still resting on my throat, I realize I want to be more than just a hookup, for once.

I want to be more than just another man's experimental phase.

Because clearly, that worked so well with the last one.

"Is this why you came?" I hiss, my walls going up as my heart starts to harden, protecting itself once more. I push back against him, escaping his hold.

Duncan catches his breath. "What?"

"To fuck with me some more? Lead me on to think you want me, and then just push me away? Take me up into the bedrooms and get me all worked up then leave me hard and wanting, only to parade me around in public and pretend we're just bandmates. That this is just a job." The words come of their own accord, and I can't stop them. It's like the dam has finally been broken, and years worth of pain surges forth.

I know it's not all about Duncan.

But he's here, and he broke me.

So, I suppose this is it. It's sink or swim, and I am tired of fucking treading water.

I don't want to drown anymore in the Black Sea.

"Is that what you think of me?" he asks, his eyebrows furrowed. For a moment, the pain registers on his face, but it is soon replaced by something else, something I am much more familiar with.

Anger.

"That I'm some cruel asshole who wants to hurt you?"

"What I think of *you* has nothing to do with this," I hiss. I turn away from him, heading for the door.

He grabs me by my wrist, his grip tight and warm, and I hate how it makes my blood rush, how his nails digging into my skin makes my damn cock throb.

"Felix..." His tone is not accusatory, but it is a

warning.

I shake him off, hating the feeling of emptiness that sweeps over me because he is no longer touching me.

"Felix, please, just hear me out, okay?" Duncan's voice is strained.

"Why? So you can spout more philosophical shit to me and make me want to be a better fucking person and then lead me on, only to tell me you don't want this..." The words are like knives as I speak them, as I try to shove the anger, the pain, and the overwhelming need to cry down into the pits of my stomach, but it's no use.

I don't even think a drink can fix this.

Or several.

"I don't know how to do this, Felix! I don't—"

"Do what?" I snap. I don't move to leave, because I am a serious glutton for punishment.

A masochist in love.

Carnage is the only thing I know.

"I don't know how to do *this*," he growls, pointing between us, his voice shaking. "I've never been with anyone... like you."

I scoff at his words. They slice me like

daggers, ripping through flesh. His hold on my wrist lessens, but he doesn't drop my hand.

His gaze captures mine, and I almost feel like an asshole.

Almost.

"What is that supposed to mean?" I bite.

Duncan's thumbs rubs my raised vein, softly.

His gaze implores me as my heart beats so loudly in my chest I think he can hear it.

This... this is where I die.

Because this is where Duncan McKay breaks my heart, and I'll never be able to recover.

"You know who you are, Felix. Good or bad, you know who you are, and you accept that. I don't..." His voice cracks. "I don't know who I am. I thought I did, for a while... I was Duncan McKay, drummer of *Hollow Pointe*. I was Duncan McKay, husband and father. But now..."

"But now, what?" I ask, my own voice slipping with the truth as I await his words.

"I feel like I'm discovering myself all over again. With you." Duncan reaches out, settling his hand on my neck once more, but he doesn't grip me. He slides his fingers back, teasing the trimmed hair at the nape of my neck gently.

It's a strange sort of feeling, given that there

is nothing *soft* about Duncan's looks.

The man is built like a brick wall, large and ominous with his dark hair, speckled with strands of gray, and deep brown eyes that glitter with gold and amber in the light.

My gaze settles on his shiny, silver lip ring.

And for once in my life, I don't want to fight.

So, I don't.

I reach out, settling my hand on his neck, and I pull Duncan McKay to my lips like he is oxygen, and I am deprived.

I move my lips slowly against his, savoring every sensation; the pillowy soft texture of his mouth, the metallic taste of his lip ring, the warm, smooth texture of his tongue.

I slide my free hand around his tree trunk waist, but I don't dig my nails in. Instead, I smooth my fingers over the silk of his shirt, rhythmically drawing lines across his muscles, where I can feel the faintest dip of skin, of his hipbones.

I lead him softly, slowly, and he follows me without question, his entire body *relaxing* against me as he settles his free hand on my hip, slowly sliding it back to rest just above my ass.

Heat envelopes us both as we give in to the

fire that exists between us, the one that I am certain is impossible to distinguish.

"I don't know how to do this, either," I whisper against his lips. I close my eyes and he rests his forehead against mine. "I don't know how to be the kind of person you deserve." My voice comes out shaky, nervous. "But I want to be."

Duncan looks at me with glassy amber eyes. "You are," he whispers as he kisses me again, forcing his tongue in my mouth, biting at my steel, causing my cock to twitch.

He presses his body against mine, and I can't argue with him. Not when his mouth travels to my neck, biting and sucking at my flesh, or as his hands slide over my body, exploring it with newfound interest.

His fingers slowly, deftly trace the outline of my cock as he continues his assault on my neck.

"You need to tell me," I choke out, needing to be one hundred percent with him before I completely cross a line he isn't comfortable with. "If you want me to stop. I'll stop."

The words feel strange on my tongue, because I don't know how to take things slow.

Duncan stops his assault on my neck, looking

into my eyes. "Do you want *me* to stop?"

"Oh fuck, no," I whisper, signing my damn tombstone.

Duncan smiles, the corners of his lips lighting up his eyes as his fingers slowly unbutton my pants and I think this is it.

If we do this, there is no going back.

Duncan slides his palm against my cock, the thin fabric of my boxers the only thing separating us, and I look up at him, noting his dilated pupils.

My breath catches in my throat as he stares at me with an intense gaze, his fingers slipping through the thin slit of my boxers.

I close my eyes in ecstasy as his fingers slide against my swollen head, and his hand wraps around my cock.

My shoulders tense as an involuntary moan escapes my throat.

"You like this?" he asks curiously. "Me touching you, like this?"

I nod furiously. "Fuck yes, but I'd like it better if it was your mouth." I say the words, not thinking twice about them, but once they are out there, I immediately regret them.

Damn fucking no filter Felix!

I know I should slow things down, let him take the lead, but it's hard. I don't know how to *not* be in control, when it comes to *this.*

Duncan squeezes me tightly, his thumb pressing into my slit.

"Oh really?" he teases, his voice dark as he nibbles at the shell of my ear with his teeth. His lip ring rattles against my skin, causing a shiver to race down my spine.

Duncan backs me up against the wall, pressing my body against it, my cock warm in his solid grip, throbbing with need.

Between the dark tone of his voice, the feel of his hand wrapped around me, and his lips on my neck, I don't even know if I will make it if he *does* take me by mouth.

Jesus Christ!

"Uh huh..." Words are difficult at the moment, and my faculties are slowly disappearing.

Any minute, I'll become a fucking vegetable if he keeps this up.

"Well, then, I suppose we should give the spoiled brat what he wants, or he'll probably throw another temper tantrum, right?" Duncan chastises me, and it ignites feelings within me that make me want to scream for mercy.

I want to come so fucking bad, and the way he's touching me, slowly squeezing and stroking my cock, I think I'm not that far off.

I twist beneath him, thrusting my cock in his palm, seeking the friction.

"Get on your fucking knees," I growl, adding a "Please" for good measure, because I don't want to sound like a complete asshole.

Duncan chuckles as he slides down my legs slowly. "Maybe this will kill your fucking attitude," he purrs, and before I can say anything, he lets go of me.

The crisp, cool air kisses my skin and my cock twitches.

And just when I think perhaps he's changed his mind, I feel the onslaught of his wet, warm tongue, and the world around me disappears.

CHAPTER 19

Duncan

Knowing the press is on the other side of the hall only adds to the thrill of what I am about to do.

I've never considered myself an exhibitionist by any means, but public sex has always been something of a kink for me.

Though I can say, despite my limited experience with Issax, I've never sucked dick before, but I am not about to back down now.

Not when Felix is practically putty from just my *licking* him.

I'm half concerned he's having a stroke, and

will have to re-learn English all over again by the time I'm done with him.

Which, honestly, is pretty satisfying for my ego, given the fact that I'm no longer *testing the waters.*

I'm diving right fucking in.

A plethora of thoughts try to dissuade me, try to poison my resolve.

What if I hate it?

What if I suck at sucking dick and I can't get him off?

God, that would be embarrassing on so many levels.

Just think about what you like, and try to emulate that.

I tell myself just because I've never done it, doesn't mean I don't know how.

I mean, it's not rocket science, right?

I let out a breath as I grab him by the base, holding him still as I run my tongue over him slowly from base to tip, his taste exploding into my mouth. I shiver, entranced, as I watch his body shudder at the contact.

He reaches out, sliding his fingers into my hair, grabbing my locks with ferocity before easing up slightly.

I can't deny that it's hot as hell, and so is the way he thrusts his cock in my face, against my lips, the sounds of desperation ebbing from his chest.

"Open your fucking mouth," he growls, and my own cock throbs with response.

Normally, Felix's attitude would piss me off and I would put him in his place.

Reprimand him for being a spoiled little brat with an attitude problem, but this?

This is another level, and I can't deny it's fucking *hot*.

I don't even think twice about obeying his command, like he's somehow unlocked something within me that I wasn't sure existed until this exact moment.

Without thinking I open wide, taking him into my mouth until I almost gag.

"Oh fuck," Felix curses, falling forward. His free hand hits the wall behind me as he steadies himself. "Your mouth feels fucking amazing." His breath shudders from his mouth as he rears his hips back, then thrusting into my mouth until he hits the back of my throat.

I do gag, but it isn't an unpleasant feeling. Strangely, it's arousing as fuck and I let out a groan of approval as I cup his covered balls with one hand, using my free hand to squeeze the sizeable tent in my pants.

Felix curses again as he snaps his hips back, building a rhythm as he fucks my mouth until drool starts to pool down my chin.

I roll my tongue around him, finding the secret steel beneath his base, flicking the barbell with my tongue and the sound that escapes his throat is like music to my ears.

"Show me your cock," he hisses, thrusting into the back of my throat so I can't speak.

I gaze up at his lustful expression, at the way he bites his lip, his lip piercing glinting in the light, and I get an idea.

I jiggle his piercing, eliciting another groan and he sucks in a breath, cursing once more.

"Show. Me. Your. Cock," he grits through his teeth. He adds a *please* that is so desperate, I don't have the will to keep fucking with him.

Though, I can't say I dislike seeing Felix at my mercy one fucking bit.

I do as he asks once more, releasing his balls as I pop open my buttons, and unzip my own pants.

I fumble with the fabric of my boxers,

because I'm already hot and moist enough that I'm sticking to the fabric, but the moment my cock springs free, Felix curses again.

"I want you to touch that beautiful cock of yours," he hisses, adding an awkward "please" again which only makes my heart beat faster.

Felix is a demanding person, that much I know, but he is also exceptionally perceptive of those around him.

I slide my hand around my cock, which throbs with renewed arousal as he ceases his thrusts, my mouth still full of his cock.

"I'm going to fuck your mouth while I watch you stroke that pretty cock," he bites, snapping his hips again until he makes me gag. "And then I'm going to watch you come with my cock down your throat."

Tears pool in my eyes and I have never wanted to please a person like *this* in my life.

Because I've always been the one in control.

Of Issax, of Marci.

But I know as Felix slowly fucks my mouth, his blue eyes blazing with fire as he watches me, that I am *not* in control here.

I groan around his throbbing member, pulling back just enough that I can suck and nibble at his cockhead, pressing my tongue into his salty slit.

Felix grabs me by the hair as I stroke myself.

I'm already so wet from my own precum, my strokes come easy.

"That's it, you're doing so fucking good," he growls as he thrusts himself back in my open, needy mouth. His words are dirty, in tone, and in sound, as his accent colors each word.

I don't hate this at all.

Don't get me wrong, I like *getting* head just as much as anyone, but *giving* it is a whole other experience.

"Fuck, I'm coming," he cries as his thrusts turn erratic, and I cry out an incoherent mumble around his cock as I slide my hand over my exploding dick to avoid making a mess on my expensive clothes.

Seriously, I doubt these digs are machine washable.

Felix's hand loosens its grip in my hair as his cock pulses, filling my mouth with warm, thick cum.

Before I can think twice about it, I swallow his release and he pulls back, spilling a few drips across my lips, beside my lip ring.

I look up at him as reality sets in, feeling like the air has left my lungs.

I absentmindedly lick Felix's cum from my lips, watching as he tries to catch his breath.

My cock deflates as he looks at me for a moment, before tucking his cock back in his pants, heading for the bathroom without a word, his breaths heavy.

Leaving me alone, on the floor, with my aching knees and tight, tense thigh muscles, my own release dripping down my shaft.

Reality settles on me and I know without a doubt, I am not straight.

Not by a long shot.

I might have thought I was, because I lived a mostly straight lifestyle, but the truth is collecting in my hand, running down my slowly deflating cock.

I enjoyed making him come.

For me.

Felix walks back into the room, with a white towel, his bright blue eyes fixating on me where I sit. With a softness that defies everything Felix Hart is known for, he kneels beside me, his gaze holding me still as he *gently* takes my cum-covered hand, cleaning every finger with the towel, and I watch him, unable to speak, or breathe right.

The tenderness in which his long, lithe, tattooed fingers stroke my fingers feels uncharacteristically intimate.

There are no words, just the silent understanding, the delicate touch that shouldn't even be possible for someone like Felix.

I should feel dirty.

I should feel ashamed, especially as Felix cleans me up.

But I only feel satisfied in a way that resonates deep within my soul, in a way I haven't felt in a long, long time.

When he's done, he pulls out his phone from his pocket, disposing of the towel in the guestroom hamper by the bed as I get up, my legs stiff, and I think I actually hear one of my knees crack, but I ignore it. I sound like a box of Rice Krispies most days when I'm *not* on my knees for mouthy rockstars.

"Press in ten. We should head out."

I nod, feeling like a damn flightless bird, as I tuck myself back into my pants, zipping up once more, and head to the bathroom to wash my hands.

I run the water, letting the warmth soothe my skin, glancing at my reflection in the brightly lit mirror.

I'm still the same me I've always been, but somehow, I'm different.

How is it that nothing has changed, when *everything* has changed?

Felix stands in the doorway, staring at me like he knows everything is different, too.

"I'm sorry," he says, his voice barely a whisper.

"Sorry for what?" I ask, confused, turning off the water.

Felix holds himself tightly, not looking at me directly. "I pushed you too hard, I should've…"

At that moment, I finally understand what is haunting Felix.

The man with an attitude, who fights and causes a scene.

The man who writes lyrics about wanting to be a shark, but being weak.

Felix does know who *he* is, but I would bet my house the people he's loved have shamed him for it, as well as what he likes. What he wants.

God, I've been so fortunate to have been married to someone who let me be myself.

Familiar lyrics echo in my brain as I look at him.

My carnage is yours to take.

And take it, I will Felix. All of it.

I pat my semi-dry hands on my thighs as I approach him in the doorway, grabbing him by the hips once more, careful to keep my touch light. I get the feeling that as brash and feisty as Felix is, that it's mostly just a mask. A wall to protect himself.

I want to be a shark, but I'm fucking weak.

"I'm okay," I whisper, stroking the side of his hip gently. He shifts under my touch, but I don't miss how his muscles loosen.

"Shit, Felix, I lived through the eighties and the nineties. It's going to take a lot more than a rough blowjob to scare me away."

The faintest hint of a smile forms on his face, and melts my heart. He doesn't look at me, instead jiggling his lip ring.

"Promise?" he whispers, his accent prominent as his facade dissolves. The vulnerability in his voice breaks me.

I turn him by his neck, forcing him to look up at me. I kiss him softly, whispering against his lips, "Promise."

Felix breaks away, nodding. He looks up at me with soft, glassy blue eyes that remind me of the ocean at midnight. "I think... I think we should just take things slow for now. Keep this to ourselves, of course."

Something about his words, the fragility in the way they are spoken makes my heart break for Felix.

I know it should go without saying, but I can also appreciate him putting himself out there, defining some sort of boundary. Plus, it's probably a good idea to take things slow, if only for my sake, but a part of me wants to argue with him that there's nothing to be ashamed of, because I understand he's likely been hiding this part of himself for a long time. Not just from the public, but maybe even from himself.

At the same time, though, part of me *wants* to shout the truth from the rooftops now that I've come to understand the truth about myself. This newly discovered puzzle piece that feels like it's been missing and it's finally home.

I'm bisexual.

The word is heavy, but it is also cathartic.

It's taken me thirty years and a spoiled brat to realize it, but now that I know...

It's startling to think I didn't. That I'd been in such denial, I didn't see it.

But all I can say is, "Okay," and nod like an idiot.

Felix's vulnerable expression is replaced by a devilish smirk as he channels the Felix everyone knows, tucking away the Felix only very few have seen, I'm sure.

Hiding away the Felix he really is.

"It's showtime," he says as he heads for the door, leaving me and my heart alone, ravaged once more.

After the interviews commence, the party begins.

I look at my watch, noting it's nearing eleven thirty, and I'm not sure how much longer this engagement is supposed to go.

Felix doesn't leave my side, and I notice he's a bit skittish, but I'm not entirely sure it isn't from what transpired between us earlier.

Then I catch his gaze as it falls on a waitress's tray, on a glass of champagne.

"You want a drink." I say the words solidly, not as a question, because if there is one thing I do know, it's the signs of chemical dependency.

Because I've been through it, myself, not to mention with Issax.

"I don't," he denies, but there isn't any weight to the words.

"You've been staring at the champagne glasses all evening," I press, turning to raise an eyebrow.

"No, really I'm good." His voice is a bit shaky, and I know he's struggling.

"A week ago you were walking into rehearsal still drunk from the night before. What changed?" I eye Jinger and the other guys on tour as they all toast their glasses together, laughing and dancing.

Felix shrugs. "Some old man told me to get my shit together when I showed up drunk to work. Seemed like a good idea at the time."

I smirk, shaking my head.

Little shit.

"You don't have to stay, you know. I'm sure they won't give a shit if you leave," he says.

"What about you?" I ask, leaning over the veranda railing. The air is hot, humid for this time of night, but I can't deny it feels nice.

"What about me?" Felix asks, rubbing his

hands together. He takes his stance next to me, his arm brushing against mine.

It's just our proximity, but it feels like more.

Like a private language only we know.

"Would you give a shit if I left?" I ask.

Felix glances at me from beneath my lashes. "Maybe."

I shake my head, smirking at his petulance.

He is such a fucking *brat*.

"Well, it is a school night, so I probably should get home. My kid was just suspended, so staying out partying probably won't get me father of the year."

Felix nods, understanding befalling his face. "I'll, uh... walk you to your car?" He says the words as if he doesn't understand them, as if they are brand new.

And maybe to him, they are.

"Sure," I reply, watching as a nearby photographer takes our picture.

Felix leads us off the property to the parking garage.

Because of course, these assholes have a full on hanger for all their pricey cars.

My truck sticks out like a sore thumb, but a part of me is proud of that.

In a sea of Bentleys and Porsches, my baby looks like damn Godzilla.

Felix stops in front of my car, sliding his hands in his pockets. "I, uh... guess I'm going to head home, too. Call it a night."

I give him a soft smile. "Good choice."

Felix's lips twist with the ghost of a smile and he grunts, "Yeah, I guess."

Before I can say my goodbyes, he nods. "See you at rehearsal, McKay."

I know we're in public and anyone can see us, as well as hear us if they are close enough, but damn if I don't want to kiss him right now.

To give him the assurance he craves because it's clear to me he never got it. From anyone.

But the last thing I want to do is draw more attention to Felix, in a negative way.

Despite his sexual antics, it's clear that the truth isn't well known. Not to mention, I have barely grasped my own freaking awakening, so I know kissing Felix right now is a terrible idea.

But that doesn't mean I don't want to.

Instead, I pull him in for a hug. Hugs are normal, those can't be dissected, right? Bandmates hug each other all the time.

Felix's body stiffens, as if he's surprised by the

motion, but within seconds, his entire body relaxes as he brings up his arms, his hands slapping me on the shoulder like we're nothing more than bros.

I feel his body tremble against mine and I squeeze him a little tighter before letting go, hoping it's enough.

Because for now, it's going to have to be.

CHAPTER 20

Felix

Samson meows at me petulantly as I strum away on my guitar.

While I usually write late at night, this morning when I woke up, I couldn't get the words out of my head. Instead of fighting it, I sat down in my studio, busted out my guitar, and started to play.

And the words came easily, much easier than they have in the past.

But one glance at my clock tells me it is a half hour past this little orange demon's snack time, which means he's likely to murder me in my sleep if I don't feed him.

"You are impossible, you know that? A total muse killer." Samson stares at me with disdain.

I haven't had a pet since I was probably a kid. I never saw the point, being as I'm gone so much, and I realize as he voices his very important opinion on his starvation, that I need to figure *something* out.

I can always get my regular housekeeper to take care of him, but something about leaving him with someone else makes me feel paranoid, not to mention, I kind of like having him around. It's less lonely.

"What do you think, huh? Think you can handle a stadium tour?"

Samson looks at me with a murderous gaze and lets out a high-pitched meow.

As long as you feed me on time, I don't care where we are.

I roll my eyes, figuring it's best to sate the beast before he gets too ornery, and drop my newly gifted guitar from Duncan on the couch.

Samson follows me out to the kitchen, and I ready his bowl, which reads *Bad Kitty* with a fishbone skeleton.

Though he isn't really bad, at all.

More like badass.

Hey, if Taylor Swift can cart her cats around the world, surely I can bring him to a couple shows.

After I've slaved in the kitchen to bring my feline god their offering of canned tuna, I take a look around my open space, which is practically so pristine, it doesn't look like anyone lives here.

In fact, it looks more like a museum than a house.

When I bought it, I hadn't really thought about the size. Everyone worth their salt had a huge ass house that was decked out to look like a space station, right?

Not to mention, I was constantly touring and traveling and didn't really plan on spending much time at home, so what did it matter what it looked like?

But this last year, things have slowed down a lot.

Black Sea bombed, and press has been at an all time low, and suddenly, I found myself alone in this massive house.

Except for the parties, of course. The parties Sully threw because he said my house was perfect for them, and it would go right along with the *image* I am presenting to the masses.

Then Lou came to me with the news of the *Pillars of Rock* tour, and I couldn't say no.

I was getting too antsy in this damn place, and Sully's ying-yang bullshit was starting to grate on my last fucking nerve. So, of course, I said yes.

But now, as I stand here, I realize the reason I've never felt at home here is because I've never *made* it a home.

Everything in this place was designed by someone else.

Everything, except for my studio.

Even my bedroom was designed and decorated by someone else.

Someone whose presence seems to haunt me like a ghost everywhere I go.

Time off isn't something I'm used to.

But Lou insisted we all break for a couple days and come back to the studio refreshed for one more rehearsal, then next week is all sound checks and preparation for the kickoff show.

It's as Lou says, "The calm before the storm."

Samson meows in happiness, and I grin. "You're absolutely right, Samson. I should decorate the place more. I think I'll do that. Haven't been shopping in a while, and it is good for the soul."

Samson licks his food, which is as good a confirmation as any, and I make the split decision. I grab my keys, head for my bike, and take off for some retail rewards.

After all, I think I deserve some new shiny things.

I ANXIOUSLY AWAIT my venti mocha with an extra shot of espresso, feeling a little better about my stylish new purchases.

Especially, the coffin-shaped pet bed and the matching coffin cat tower I bought for Samson while we tour.

Okay, and maybe I picked up some things for myself, too, of course.

And maybe I even picked up some more pieces to add to Duncan's capsule wardrobe.

Including a weathered and distressed Slayer shirt and some vintage acid wash jeans I know he'll look fucking amazing in.

The barista calls my order out, and I make

my way with all my bags in tow to grab the large cup of God's nectar, when a voice stops me dead in my tracks.

"Well, would you look at that…"

I tighten my fingers around the cardboard barrier as I contemplate whether I should turn around or not.

I could just ignore my former not-boyfriend, walk away like he is truly the scum on the bottom of my shoe.

And in all honesty, that is what I *should* do.

But Sullivan Reign's voice is like some twisted form of hypnosis.

I couldn't ignore it, even if I wanted to.

I turn to see him standing there in his tight jeans and his stupid Balenciaga shirt that doesn't look as expensive as he thinks it does.

"Sully," I murmur, and I take a sip of my drink, not moving from my spot.

Sully has the audacity to smirk at me, exposing his diamond-encrusted canine.

"I almost thought you were a fucking mirage. You never leave the dungeon during the day."

I shrug as he approaches me. "Last I checked, I didn't have to run my schedule by you. Seeing as you ain't in the fucking band anymore."

He stops inches away from me, glancing at the baristas then back at me.

He scoffs, chuckling as if he truly finds this interaction funny.

"Something you want, Sullivan?" I bite as I watch him lick his lips.

"An apology would be nice. Seeing as you decided to air our fucking dirty laundry to everyone within a five mile radius the other night. My manager has had a field day with trying to squelch those nasty rumors."

An apology?

From me?

This asshole has lost his damn mind!

"Really? I don't recall." I brush past him, shoulder checking him.

Sully grabs my wrist, and immediately, I stop. A shiver runs through me as he presses his thumb against my vein with a force that tells me he isn't in the mood for playing games.

Games I used to love once upon a time, but now the touch feels wrong.

It makes me feel gross, like I want to fucking throw up.

I yank my wrist from him. "What's your

fucking problem, man?" I bite, challenging his space.

Sully sneers at me. "You think you can play stupid with me, Felix, I know you better than you fucking know yourself."

I get in his face, sneering right back. My anger boils beneath my skin like a volcano waiting for the right moment to erupt.

"Think just because you replaced me that you can write me off and fuck me over? And that I wouldn't do something about it?"

I grind my jaw, fixing his gaze with my own hard glare. "Fuck you over? Is that the narrative you're going with, Sully? I'm the one that god damn *made* you. I brought you into this fame, and I can take you out of it, just as easy."

I know I should walk away. But the pain, the anger, and the need to make him *hurt* like he hurt me wins out.

Sully pushes me, and it's like a hundred moments breaking through the barrier.

All the fights that ended in fucking.

All the fucking that ended in fights

And all the pussy in between he paraded around because he was too *scared* to be seen in public kissing someone with dick.

Kissing *me.*

My fist connects with his damn fine jaw, and then his fist connects with my eye, and it's a blur of fists and curses as Sully and I are pulled apart. The sound of cameras clicking is loud, and I know this will be all over the news outlets within minutes, and I chastise myself internally.

"What the fuck, Sullivan?" another voice calls, a man I don't recognize.

When he grabs Sully, I can tell by his suit and his baby face he's corporate, which means he's probably Sully's new manager.

Now that he's separated from the band, of course he'd decide to fly solo.

The manager asks us to leave as my phone goes off, and I sigh in exasperation as I see Lou's name flash on the screen.

I dig Lou's card out of my wallet and hand it to the manager as Sullivan's manager shoves him out the door.

"I'm sorry about that, but, uh... if there's anything I can do, please let my manager know, okay?" I say as I gather myself, my bags, and my half spilled coffee, and head out the door, answering the phone.

"Yeah?"

"What the fuck were you thinking?" Lou hollers on the other end.

I don't even bother playing dumb with Lou. It's best to just address the situation and get on with it.

My eye hurts like a bitch, and so do my knuckles, and the anger is still boiling inside of me like lava, but I answer him. "Well, for starters, he insulted me."

"Everyone insults you, Felix. Last I checked, you didn't fucking start a *brawl* with everyone of those individuals at four pm in a damn Starbucks."

"Consequences have actions," I say as I tie my bags off and secure them to the back of my bike carrier.

"Yes, they do, and now, I've got a pissed off agent, an angry Starbucks manager, and damage control to whip in to shape so you can have a fucking successful show next week," Lou hisses. "Why can't you ever just let shit go? For once in your life, be the better fucking man, Felix."

Lou's words cut me deeper than any knife.

What am I supposed to do?

Let the man treat me like shit *in public* where people are watching?

I'm not some weak little thing he can just—"

Once he starts spouting off more words that are incoherent, and that I don't care for, I sigh and respond, "I got to go, Lou."

I hang up as the anguish starts to spill over. My sights settle on a bar a few doors over, and I think that maybe a stiff drink will quiet the awful thoughts threatening to infiltrate my sanity.

You are trash.

Sully knows it, Lou knows it, you know it.

I swallow harshly as I try to fight the words, fight the desire to drown myself in the Black Sea, in the bottom of a glass.

I turn the engine on, trying to drown out the impulse, the voices in my head that tell me we can forget about it.

I can call up Jinger and Page Six and forget all about fucking Sullivan Reign and his cruel touch, his loathsomely smutty voice.

The song that comes over my radio pulls me back to the here and now, as Duncan's deep voice croons about being a loose cannon, and I know exactly what it is I need.

CHAPTER 21

Felix

I KNOCK TWICE before a shirtless Duncan answers the door. My gaze settles on his broad shoulders, the coarse, thick mat of dark brown and gray hair decorating his chest, his chestnut hair and eyes like a beacon in the dark.

"Felix? Is everything—"

My throat feels tight, as the last several years converge on me all at once like an avalanche.

"No," I reply, shaking my head. My voice slips, which only happens when I am not in control of who I am *supposed* to be.

My vision blurs as I try to fight the tears, but they are stronger than I am.

"No, I'm not okay."

Duncan's thick eyebrows knit together as he pulls me into his arms immediately. His hold is tight, strong, and I crumble like a deck of cards.

"It's okay... Come on in." His voice stern and authoritative as he leads me into his house. Though there's an edge to his voice that is different than all the other times he's been the bearer of hard truths.

I know if there is one person who will be straight with me, who will tell me the truth, no sugar, it's Duncan.

Duncan shuts the door with one hand, leading me toward the couch.

"Wh—where's B—Bobby?" I ask through sobs and sniffles.

"Spending the night at a friend's house, why?"

I sniffle, my voice shaking. "Didn't want to look a fucking mess in front of your kid. Got... got an image to uphold."

Duncan sighs and the sound is heavy as he pulls me down to the couch.

"You're not a mess, Felix."

"Yes, I am!" I sob like an absolute mess.

Is he fucking blind?

"I kn—know you s—said if I wanted to not be trash, I n—needed to not t—treat myself like it, but fuck…"

Duncan sighs as I wipe my eyes, unable to stop the onslaught of tears.

"I'm not a good person, Duncan. I'm not. I'm a fucked up piece of shit."

Another sob wracks me.

"What happened?" he asks, leaning back into the couch, pulling me with him.

I lean on his shoulder, not daring to look up at him because I don't want to see how fucked up I truly am.

I don't want to see his pity.

His fingertips trace lightly over my shoulder as he leans toward me, the scratchiness of his beard briskly brushing against my forehead.

"I wanted to ignore him. To walk away, but I couldn't." I pinch the bridge of my nose as I close my eyes.

"Who?" Duncan's voice is even, solid, like a rock.

"Sullivan fucking Reign."

"Ah." Duncan's brief utterance is full of judgment.

Maybe this was a bad idea, coming here, like this.

"Maybe I should go..." I say, shoving down the demons that are fighting for freedom. "I should—"

"You hungry?" Duncan asks as he gets up, letting me fall against the back of the couch.

I watch as he stands, pulling up his gray sweatpants to cover his hips.

I fixate my gaze on him, on the soft curves and edges of his waist, on the thick smattering of hair that covers him from chest to navel. As my gaze travels up to his face, I can't help but appreciate the sight of him like this.

Duncan is like a diamond, with so many contrasting facets, each one equally as blinding and sharp in design as the last.

It's hard to believe the same Duncan McKay who used to sport a lip ring and mascara is the same man who can throw me over his shoulder like a ragdoll, who is also somehow the same man who left Hollywood for a house in the suburbs with a fucking white picket fence.

And somehow he's the same man who can quiet all the noise inside of me.

I've been digging through coal for so long, I didn't know diamonds still existed.

I've burned for so long through fires self-inflicted.

I'm going to have to write that one down.

"I, uh…"

"Because I'm starving," Duncan says nonchalantly as he heads for the fridge. He opens it and the light shines on his skin, illuminating his side profile, his sweatpants sliding off of him once more to reveal a softer definition.

Most of the men in my life, aside from Lou are all coke thin or so muscular you could bounce a fucking quarter off their abs.

There's something pleasantly comforting about a man who carries himself with the confidence Duncan has.

Confidence I wish I had.

"I'll warn you, though, my kid is a much better cook than I am. Though, I make a mean grilled cheese."

I nod like an idiot, a small laugh escaping my throat. The last time I'd been here, he made some sort of buffalo chicken dip, and I swear to God, it smelled like heaven.

Of course, that might've had something to do with the man who made it, and not the dish itself, since I left before I could even get a taste.

"I can't remember the last time someone made me a grilled cheese. Probably my mom when I was sick, when I was a kid."

I get up from the couch, slowly making my way to the kitchen as I watch Duncan get the ingredients together.

Watch the way his shoulders move as he spreads butter over two pieces of crusty bread, the way the shadows fall on his face.

God, he's aged so fucking well.

He might've been positively delicious when he was younger, but now...

I swallow harshly and try not to stare.

"You don't talk about your parents much. Not even in articles."

I take a seat on one of his barstools at the counter, focusing on his prepwork.

"That's because there's nothing to talk about. My dad left when I was eleven. Went out for a pack of cigarettes, never came back. Mom never recovered and spent the remainder of my life at home working double shifts so we could survive."

Duncan turns on a burner, letting the griddle heat up.

"Dad tried to come back a couple years later, after I had my first hit. Looking for money, and I gave it to him. Never heard from him again. Mom... she's out reliving her lost years in Europe somewhere. Fuck if I know where."

"I'm sorry," he says, dropping a buttered piece of bread on to the griddle. It sizzles when it makes contact, screeching at first, then fading to nothing.

"It's fine. It is what it is."

"And Sully?" Duncan presses some cheese onto the unbuttered side, then tops it with a fresh piece of buttered bread.

"Sully, Eddie, and Corpse were hired to be my band after my first album. When I started touring. He wasn't the first guy I—"

Duncan moves back against the counter as he turns the burner down, letting the sandwich heat slowly.

"He made the pain feel better. For a while. Then I wanted more, and he—"

"Didn't want the same thing?" Duncan asks

as he flips the sandwich. The sizzle screams as the fresh buttered bread hits the hot surface, fading within seconds to nothing again.

"Not really, I guess. In the end, anyway. He left, and I was a mess. But somehow, I'm the bad guy, you know? I'm the one who's a problem for *him*."

Duncan flips the sandwich once more, pressing it with a spatula into the griddle, making the butter sizzle longer.

"And then today when I saw him, he started his fucking gaslighting bullshit, and I snapped."

I close my eyes, shaking my head.

"His new manager was there, and I'm sure by now it's on everyone's TikToks. Lou was pissed."

I open my eyes to see a plate of freshly made grilled cheese in front of me, and my stomach growls.

Duncan sets to fixing himself a sandwich as I take a bite out of mine, and it's amazing.

Hot, melty, and satisfying. I can't help but groan in satisfaction.

"This fucking slaps, Duncan."

The way his eyebrows lift, surprised, but somewhat joyful tells me he really thinks this is mediocre.

But nothing Duncan McKay does is mediocre.

I'm absolutely certain of it.

"Lou's just grumpy because you make him work for his paycheck." Duncan flashes me with a half smile. "Believe me, I know."

"But I don't want to be a problem. I really don't. I just... want to make my music and be fucking happy, you know?"

I take another bite of my sandwich, reveling once more in the perfection of the toasted bread and warm, satisfying cheese.

Fuck me sideways, this shit is *lit*.

"I know," Duncan says as he plates his sandwich, taking a seat next to me.

He swivels a bit on his chair, his knee knocking into mine.

The next words out of my mouth are barely audible, almost a whisper.

"For a minute I thought... There was a bar a couple doors down, and I wanted to go and—" The words stick in my throat, and won't dislodge.

Duncan looks at me as he takes a bite of his sandwich. "But you didn't."

His words are heavy on my soul, but they are also freeing.

I could have gone down the same beaten path, but I didn't.

Shimmering, sparkling, this land of diamonds and jewels

Offering me a chance to shine

Glittering and enticing, this land of milk and honey

Never have I wanted so badly to call you mine

"I didn't," I say softly,

"You want my two cents?" Duncan asks as he devours his grilled cheese in practically one bite.

"Sure."

"I think Sullivan Reign is a fucking idiot. And he's a terrible musician."

I can't help but laugh. "You know, he idolizes you, right? God, he was always talking about how good you are. That's why I was such an ass when we first met. You reminded me of him, and I was pissed."

Duncan swivels his chair toward me, his dark gaze capturing mine.

I look at him, the way his dark hair falls in his face, the way his scruff fades into a thick beard, the sliver of silver hiding beneath his beard, embedded in his lips.

Absentmindedly, I reach out and flick it with my fingers.

Duncan grabs my hand, pressing his lips to my fingers. "And now? Do I still piss you off?"

His thumb presses into my wrist, like Sully always did when he was trying to make me listen.

You just need to be broken, Felix. You can be a good boy if you want to be.

His words echo in my head, and I realize I was never going to be good enough for Sully.

Ever.

I'd always be waiting for him to throw me a fucking bone, coveting the scraps between his romances with Hollywood's hottest harlots.

And he'd somehow tide me over with those scraps and make me feel like I didn't deserve the trash he fed me.

Duncan's thumb gently strokes my vein, and I exhale.

"How did you do it?" I ask, curling my fingers underneath his jaw. His facial hair against my palm is rough, and I grip his jaw, forcing him to look at me. "How did you walk away?"

Duncan's gaze implores mine. "I watched my

friend spiral out of control, and I didn't... I didn't do anything to stop him." Duncan's voice shakes, and I can see the tears on the verge of his confession.

"Then I found him. He slit his wrists, and—" Duncan closes his eyes and my heart breaks for him.

God, I can't imagine.

When he opens his eyes, he looks at me softly. "I knew I loved music, and I loved my wife—we weren't married yet, but I thought maybe—"

Duncan sighs. "Marci always said, all you need is ten seconds to be brave. After ten seconds, it becomes the past, and all you have is the future."

I swivel in my chair, knocking my knee into his as I remove my hand from his, stacking our plates together.

"Ten seconds? That's it?" I ask as I slip down from the barstool, carrying the plates to the sink.

"Yeah. Whenever I'm freaking out, I take a deep breath, and count to ten."

I turn to look at him, sitting there. Looking at me.

"You didn't count to ten when your car died."

Duncan smirks. "I fuck up, too, you know. No one is perfect."

I have to disagree with him.

And just like that, he shrugs, changing the subject.

"I want to show you something," he says, nodding for me to follow him.

When I dropped him and his kid off, I hadn't really stayed long. Just long enough to attempt to play a song or two on the couch. Then I'd kissed him, and freaked him out and...

"Sure."

I follow Duncan through the hall as he shows me the bathroom, the guest room, Bobby's room, an open lounge, his bedroom, and lastly, his music studio and workshop.

In comparison to my two story design piece, his spacious ranch feels so much larger.

It's full of color, and comfort.

And it's *lived* in.

There are hoodies over the lounge couch, and dirty glasses on the kitchen counter, and a sink full of pots and pans.

There are clothes overflowing out of the hamper at the end of the hall.

The bed in his bedroom isn't even made.

Duncan leans against the doorframe of his workshop, his signature sweat and Old Spice scent hitting me, and I don't even hide the way I breathe it in.

"You're going to be okay, you know," he says softly, his breath hot on my neck.

I turn to lean into him. "With you, yeah. I think I am," I reply as I lean up and kiss him.

He doesn't falter or shrink back this time. Instead, he slides his fingers into my hair, pushing me against the doorframe with his body. His chest brushes against my hot pink Def Leopard tee, and it doesn't take much for me to submit.

Because when Duncan McKay touches me, it's salvation.

His free hand settles on my hip and I slide my right hand down his bare back, slipping it below the waistband of his sweats, over his ass.

He doesn't push me away.

Instead, he grinds his solid cock against me and I grow hard.

A desperate moan escapes my throat as I slide my free hand over his waist, his stomach, rubbing the soft, pliable skin. I groan as he opens his mouth, his tongue breaching my mouth, his lip ring clinking against my own.

I skim my hand up his abdomen. Where there should be muscles, there is only squishy, soft skin and a sprinkle of coarse hair against my palm.

Duncan's kiss deepens as his hands explore my body, slipping underneath my shirt as they course over my stomach.

I stroke the skin of his abs with my palm, liking the feel of his skin against mine.

"You make everything okay," I whisper.

Duncan takes my lips once more, pulling me back across the hall, toward his bedroom, and I follow him like a lamb to the slaughter, both of us kissing, touching, exploring one another as I let him lead me.

He tugs at the edge of my shirt, and I let him pull it off of me.

I think it falls somewhere between the doorway and the bed.

I back him up against the bed, but I don't push him.

He kisses my neck, his tongue warm on my flesh as his large hands splay along the sides of my exposed hips, fingers tracing lines along my tattoos.

I groan as he nips and bites at my neck, his cock twitching against me. I push his sweats down a bit.

Duncan tenses, and I stop.

I look up at him in alarm. "Are you okay, do you want me to—"

"I haven't had sex with anyone in ten years," he blurts out.

"Oh." I nod, moving back, but I come up against the edge of the bed myself and end up falling over, embarrassingly.

Thankfully, the bed catches me, but I know that'll leave a bruise.

"I just... needed you to know that."

"We don't have to... have sex." I say the words, and they feel strange. "We can just, uh... do whatever you're comfortable with," I reassure him, despite the fact my cock is throbbing, and the thought of fucking this man makes me hot as hell.

Duncan sits on the bed next to me.

"Are you a... top or... a bottom?" he asks, his cheeks flushing. "Just curious."

I can't help but smirk. Not the direction I

thought this was going to go, but I'm happy to answer whatever questions he has.

Especially if those answers will help him with this.

Us.

"I'm vers."

"Vers?" he asks, eyebrows knit together. "What does that mean?"

"I like both. Though, I'm used to being the top."

Duncan nods, his cheeks still red. "Good to know."

I can't help but laugh a little, considering the discussion.

"I'm going to guess you're a top."

Duncan's eyebrows furrow. "What makes you say that?"

"For one, you have a bite that screams *Daddy*. In a sexy way, of course. I could totally see it."

Duncan's eyes glaze over. "Oh do, I now?" he taunts me.

I nod, my own cheeks flushing as his gaze darkens.

"You think you know me, Felix, hmmm?"

For a sliver of a second, I worry I said something wrong, but when Duncan licks his lips, grinning with grade A Daddy energy, I can't help but take his fucking bait.

"Maybe a little."

"Mhmm. Well, you might be right about one thing. I do have a history of being the one on top. But you have a bite that screams fucking brat." He slides closer to me. I look up at him with a wicked grin. "And last I checked, brats like to top from the bottom."

I cast him an aloof grin. "What can I say? I told you, I have daddy issues."

Duncan stalks me, pushing me back against the headboard until his face is inches from mine.

"Such an attitude," he whispers as he kisses me, and I can feel his grin.

"Maybe I need my mouth washed out with cock," I tease, adding an ample *daddy* for maximum effect.

Duncan doesn't flinch. Instead, he groans, slipping his tongue into my mouth as he whispers against my lips, "Then what are you waiting for?"

His tone is dark, and I don't have to be told twice.

I move my lips to his neck, sucking lightly on

the taut skin there as I settle myself in his lap. Duncan rests his hands on my hips, his fingers grabbing my ass through my jeans.

The curse that escapes his mouth sends me reeling and I grind my stiff cock against him as I let my tongue lave over his clavicle, trailing it through a sea of hair and skin across his chest, down his abdomen.

I crawl down his body like a fucking spider, with not enough hands to touch him everywhere I want.

I slip my fingers beneath the sides of his sweatpants and all but yank them down, eager to taste him.

The pain and worry, the intrusive thoughts... they all disappear.

Sex has always been an escape for me.

But this... It feels different.

I can feel the tremble of Duncan's body as he sucks in a breath, as his fingers seek purchase in my hair.

For a moment, I think he's going to pull me up, tell me to stop.

Leave me hard and wanting him, again.

But he doesn't.

In fact, he does the opposite.

He shoves my head and face against his half-covered groin, thrusting up as he grunts, "Don't be a fucking tease."

The grin that falls over my face is stupid.

I shouldn't *like* the force, or the command, but damn it, I fucking love it.

Something about the tone of Duncan's voice strikes a chord within me, and I think I would do *anything* for that voice.

I pull his sweats down to his knees, letting his solid cock spring free.

The last time I laid eyes on this beautiful cock, he was pleasuring himself while I fucked his mouth, and even from my angle above him, his thickness was rather sizeable.

But up close and personal, I nearly drool at the sight.

I've had my fair amount of dick, but none as thick as Duncan.

No wonder the man has the confidence of a king.

With a battering ram like that, I'd probably feel like God's fucking favorite, too.

I half worry I will asphyxiate to death, but damn, if I die sucking his cock, it's a good way to go out.

I grab him in my hand first, and note my fingers *barely* meet one another when I wrap them around him.

It's a stretch for sure, and my mind spirals, wondering what that stretch would feel like in my ass.

Fucking hell.

My cock twitches, pushing against the inside of my jeans.

I suck in a breath and count to three, flashing my gaze up at him as I lick him from base to head, sucking on the tip, dragging my lip ring along his slit.

Four. Five. Six.

"Oh my God, Felix..." he hisses, his head hitting the back of the headboard. His fingers grip my hair tighter as he thrusts his cock against my lips, and I can taste the trickles of his precum against my tongue.

Seven. Eight. Nine.

I watch his eyebrows knit together as he sucks in a breath, his gaze finding mine. I don't break it as I let out my own breath.

Ten.

In one fell swoop, I take him into my mouth, and I feel like I might actually choke.

My cock throbs and I move to adjust myself, and Duncan grunts as I lave my tongue around his solid cock, drool forming at my chin from the motion.

I groan in ecstasy as I lick and suck, all the while imagining what it would feel like to be stuffed by this perfect cock.

His hand loosens its grip in my hair, and he breathlessly calls my name.

I lose myself in the sound of his grunts, the way he breathes my name, the lightheadedness I feel as he slowly thrusts his hips up, causing his cock to hit the back of my throat.

I push his knees apart, grinding my cock into the mattress beneath me, driven by the need to fuck *something*.

Or someone, but I'm not about to turn Duncan over and rail him into the headboard just yet, given his reluctance and his natural dominance.

But God, what I wouldn't give to watch him make a mess of this bed while I fuck him senseless.

The thought drives me to deep throat him once more, humming around his cock, and he bursts like a dam, growling out a string of curses as I swallow his load like it's my favorite goddamn drink.

When he's finished, I remove my mouth from his shaft, looking up to take stock of the euphoria on Duncan's face, when I am full on knocked over, my back hitting the soft mattress.

Duncan's mouth finds mine quickly, and he shoves his tongue down my throat, kissing me like a madman as he makes haste with my pants and my aching erection.

I lick his lip ring, thrusting my cock against his hand as he fights to free me.

"You don't have to," I tell him, because it's true.

I want him, so fucking bad, but I don't want to fuck this up, either. And in my experience, most of my partners weren't the type to reciprocate or give.

They took.

But this... this bond between us is something I've never felt with anyone before.

Duncan presses his thumb into my leaking slit, and I see stars.

I watch as my cock throbs, as he brings his wet thumb up to his lip, sucking it salaciously.

The groan that leaves my mouth is desperate, and I thrust my cock up against his semi-erect cock. I want his lips wrapped around my cock, I want his tongue in my fucking ass, and I want to be stuffed like damn Thanksgiving turkey.

The desire is so much more profound than I've ever felt.

You cut me open and you make me free.
Polished like a stone
You stitch up my battle wounds
You break my fucking throne.

The feel drives me wild, and I can see the reflection of my lust in his eyes.

"I want to," he says, kissing me once more.

He grinds himself against me, taking both my wrists in just one of his large hands, and I feel like I am drowning once more. In Old Spice and feverish kisses, in blissful submission.

He's going to need more than a wardrobe.

Maybe some new equipment for his restorations.

"I want to make you feel as good as you make me feel," he whispers against my lips before taking his free hand and wrapping it around both of our cocks.

His gaze pins me and I am powerless against

the sparks flying through me as I feel him harden once more.

Christ, at this rate, I'll buy him a vacation home in the Maldives.

His strokes are slow and torturous, and I think I could die like this.

At the mercy of Duncan McKay, in his bed.

Who needs interrogation or torture when this man can drive me to the madhouse?

Here lies Felix Hart.

May I rest in peace.

"Duncan... please..." I beg, unashamed of how desperate I sound. I want to come so bad, and I'm so close.

His touch is electric, his words everything I've never known I needed.

Just as I'm about to blow, he stops, and I nearly cry out when his mouth replaces his hand, and my cock hits the back of his throat.

I come, hard and fast, his name etched in my heart, my soul, and on my lips.

He swallows my release down with ease, vacating my deflating cock, and just as I am about to expire and melt into the mattress, he resuscitates me by pushing his swollen head against my lips.

Instinctively, I open my mouth for him and he drives his big, fat cock down my throat, coming within seconds, gruffly cursing, and I see stars.

It's not as much as the first time, but it's a sweet surrender all the same.

When we're finished, we both lie there, hot and panting like we've just run a marathon.

And in a way, I guess we have.

I've never gone back-to-back like that before, not even with Sully, and the results make me feel lethargic, but also comforted.

Duncan slides his sweatpants back up, then works to redress me somewhat, which is a feat. My body is limp and I can barely move, but I feel amazing.

Better than I've felt in a long time. My eyes feel heavy and a warmth surrounds me, strong arms pulling me close.

I burrow into coarse hair and warm skin and lips that get lost in my hair. I breathe in Old Spice and sweat, and sex.

Darkness threatens to pull me under, and I let it.

CHAPTER 22

Duncan

The moment the door the dressing room shuts, Felix is practically tearing my pants off.

And I don't bother fighting him, because I can't deny I have been thinking about break time since we pulled into the studio this morning.

Knowing Eddie, Corpse, and even Lou are flitting about while Felix and I are in here, only drives my satisfaction.

I bite at Felix's lip as he slides his hand in my pants, grabbing my swollen cock. His teeth nip at my lip ring, which I've taken to wearing again, if only because it seems to be something that drives him crazy, and makes me feel younger.

Like I'm twenty again. And despite my lack of intimacy over the last decade, my cock has forgotten its age, too.

With Felix, I feel more than just young.

I feel *alive.*

With only six days until the big show, everything is falling into place.

Marci's sister will be flying in after the show, to officially take over house and kid-sitting while I pack my things and head off on this tour, which is both thrilling and a little nerve wracking.

But I'd be lying if I said I wasn't excited to perform for a stadium full of people, alongside Felix.

His fingernails dig into the flesh of my cock and I have to stifle a groan as he pushes me down onto the couch, making the pillows go flying.

My cock bobs freely as my acid wash jeans fall to my ankles.

I told Felix he didn't have to keep buying me clothes, but when I said the words, he looked like he was about to throw one of his Felix tantrums, complete with waterworks, and he actually fucking *pouted.* Then, he threatened to buy me a new car instead. So, I relented on the personal styling fees.

Who am I to deny a spoiled brat?

It doesn't take long before his hot little mouth is wrapped around me, his fingers twisting and pulling as he strokes me.

I hiss and let my eyelids fall closed.

Then my phone interrupts us, ringing with vibrancy.

Felix pauses as I grunt in defeat.

"It's Bobby, I have to take this." I sigh.

He rarely calls me, unless it's important, and already my parental worries start to swirl.

Felix bites his lip, nodding, but he doesn't move from his spot between my legs.

Instead he just lazily draws lines along the inside of my thigh, dangerously close to my cock, while he intently watches me.

"Bobby? Is everything okay?" I answer the call as I sit up, lightly pushing Felix aside so that I can stand.

He moves languidly, pulling his knee up to his chest, his tongue jiggling his lip ring.

My cock twitches as his gaze focuses on me.

"Everything is fine, Dad. I just wanted to ask when you were coming home?"

His voice is even, but I detect a hint of nerves.

"We're wrapping up in about an hour, why? Did you want to go somewhere for dinner tonight?"

"Actually, I was thinking I could make dinner, and maybe... um... maybe I could bring a friend over. To meet you, of course."

My blood chills, because I'm aware by the enunciation of the word "friend", that this kid is more than just a friend.

"What, uh... what friend?" I ask, biting my lip.

I adjust my cock in my boxers and zip my pants up, watching as Felix's bright eyes sparkle with intrigue.

I mouth my apology, but he doesn't seem to notice. He just keeps watching me with an evil grin that makes me worried he's lost his marbles or something.

"Brendan. I know I've mentioned him before, and I just, uh... I thought it would be cool to introduce you."

"Of course. It's fine. Just don't make me cook," I tease.

Bobby sighs, but it isn't annoyed.

It hides a hint of laughter.

"Obviously. I do want to make a good impression, after all. Which means you also need to be on your best behavior. I mean it, Dad. Don't be weird."

I grin as Felix gets up.

"Sounds like this kid might be more than a friend if you're giving me a warning."

"Oh my God, Dad! Just... don't. Please. Just... be chill. Please, I'm begging you."

"Noted," I say as Felix comes to stand beside me, sinking his hands into his pockets.

"We should head back," he says calmly, nodding toward the door. "Break is almost over."

"I gotta go, Bobby. I'll see you in a couple hours, okay?"

After the line goes dead, I slide my phone back in my back pocket.

"Sorry about that," I say, feeling strangely on the spot.

Felix gingerly slides his hands up underneath my Slayer shirt.

Which was also a gift along with the jeans.

His fingertips are light long my skin and he grins.

"Don't apologize. I think it's hot." He flashes me a lusty grin.

"You think everything is hot," I tease him.

"Just everything you do," he says as he kisses me lightly, barely ghosting his lips against mine. His tongue flicks at my lip ring.

"Besides, you can make it up to me later, Daddy," he teases, smacking me in the groin for added emphasis.

I curse as I force myself to think unsexy thoughts, following Felix back to the studio.

Bobby must really like this kid.

For starters, I don't know what seventeen year old wouldn't be impressed by chicken saltimbocca, but Bobby has been a basketcase about the state of the prosciutto for the last ten minutes.

"It's fine, I promise," I reassure him as I stir the *bechemel* sauce for him.

He wouldn't trust me to do anything else, he said.

"It's over-seasoned." He snuffs, just as the doorbell rings.

Bobby's eyes widen, and I can see the nerves spike.

"Hey," I say as implore his gaze. "I'm sure everything will go great, okay? Don't worry."

I'm not sure if I'm trying to convince myself or my kid, or perhaps both of us, but this is clearly important to him.

"I have to answer the door, Dad," he says, blinking rapidly.

I nod, giving him permission to do so.

"Hey," his entire voice changes the moment he opens that door. It's not sarcastic, or annoyed, but soft.

Warm, and inviting.

The kid that steps into my house smiles warmly back at Bobby, then meets my gaze.

He's tall, like Felix. Bobby's not short by any means, but I would wager this Brendan has a good couple inches on Bobby, and by his frame and obvious muscles, he's probably some sort of athlete, I'd guess.

"You must be Brendan," I say, forcing a smile, even though I think I'm more nervous than Bobby.

Bobby seems to remember I'm here, because his shoulders tense.

I turn the burner off, wiping my hands on a towel before heading over to meet the kid face to face.

He looks at me with big, round blue eyes, his surfer blondish-brown hair glistening in the chandelier light.

"Nice to meet you Mr. McKay," he replies, his deep voice like thunderstorm.

His handshake is firm, quick.

"Good handshake," I say with a grin at Bobby, who looks like he's reconsidering this whole event.

Dinner isn't as awkward, and I channel my best supportive parent costume.

I serve them both and ask Brendan genuine questions. What he likes, what his plans are after graduating this year.

How he and Bobby became "friends."

Although he answers every question thoughtfully and politely, I notice how Bobby responds to every answer of his. How he watches the way Brendan smiles, tells his stories.

No one prepares you for moments like these. The ones where you realize your kids are really growing up.

Forging relationships.

Falling in love.

I can't discern if the feelings are mutual, though. It's clear my son is smitten with Brendan, but I can't ascertain if this sweet boy is going to break his heart or not.

I also know I can't protect him forever.

Not from things like this. All I can do is be here for him, for whatever he needs.

A part of me aches, knowing I might miss some of those firsts, being on tour for the next couple months.

But I also know that at the end of this tour, Bobby will be able to go wherever his heart desires because money won't be an issue.

When dinner is over, I clean up while Bobby gives his friend a tour of the house, and I do my best to not hover, even though I desperately want to know how things are going.

They retire to the lounge to study, and I finish up with the dishes. I try to keep myself busy, but I'm antsy.

After an hour of complete silence, I give in. I head toward the lounge to see if they need anything to find they aren't in the lounge. But Bobby's door is shut.

I don't think, I just act.

I push open his door, calling out his name, and immediately, regret it.

"Oh my God, Dad!" he yelps, jumping up from his bed, face flushed.

Brendan laughs a little, awkward laugh, his hands in his lap, shaking his head.

"Doors remain open in this house!" I bite out, averting my gaze.

"Yes, sir," Brendan says as Bobby curses.

I'll let the language go for now.

"I think I should probably head out anyway. Gotta get a good night's rest so I can pass the test, right?" he says softly, trying to diffuse the tension.

I nod, my gaze catching Bobby's. "Right, it is a school night and all."

I am the worst Dad ever. Bobby is going to hate me for this.

"Walk me out?" Brendan asks, his eyebrows furrowing together, and I can see one hundred percent why Bobby has his knickers in a twist over this kid.

I know that look. The pleading, sweet gaze that would send a man to his knees.

Then I notice the prominent *hickey* on my son's neck.

I clear my throat, as Bobby nods. "Yeah, of course," he replies as he glares at me.

I step back from the doorway to let them leave.

"It was nice meeting you," I say with a fake smile, feeling like I need a damn drink.

Brendan looks me dead in the eye and says, "Pleasure was mine, Mr. McKay."

A myriad of emotions fill me from panic to pride, to fear to anxiety.

Bobby walks his 'friend' to the door, and they say their goodbyes. The moment the door shuts, Bobby groans.

"Dad, I—"

"Listen, I'm not mad—" I interupt, slowly approaching him.

Bobby sighs, running his hands over his face. "I can not do this with you, I can't. I just can't."

I stop in front of him, pulling his hands down. "You think I want to do this? This is awkward as hell for me, too, you know!"

Bobby averts my gaze. "Then let's just not and say we did, okay?" He pouts.

I shake my head. "I'd be the same way if it was a girl in there, Bobby. I know... I know you're going to do... stuff... and I'd rather you do it somewhere safe... like in this house. But—"

"Please kill me, now."

"I think we need to have a real discussion about safe sex. Like... you do know *how* to use a condom, right?"

I blush, realizing I probably should have had this discussion years ago, but I thought I had more time.

He never seemed interested in girls, and I hadn't *thought* about the possibility he was into boys, so I just assumed he wasn't interested in sex at all, and was going to be a late bloomer.

I fucked up, obviously.

I'm an awful parent.

The absolute worst.

"You should probably get tested, too, just to make sure—"

"That goes for you, too!" Bobby says, crossing his arms.

"Excuse me?"

"If you're going to start, uh... seeing people—"

"What makes you think I'm seeing someone?" I ask, dumbfounded.

Bobby huffs in annoyance. "Please. Someone

is buying you clothes, and I smelled cologne the other day when I came home."

"I wear cologne!" I defend, though I know it's flimsy.

"You don't wear Sauvage. You wear Bath and Body Works."

My mouth gapes open as he raises an eyebrow.

There is no getting out of this, and I suppose, if I expect him to live up to my expectations, I should be the one to set an example.

"Fine. We'll go together." I cross my arms.

"Fine." Bobby raises his chin.

"And I'm buying you a pack of condoms. Don't always assume the other guy is carrying them."

Bobby rolls his eyes. "I have condoms, Dad. I'm not an idiot."

"Oh," I say, feeling a strange sense of pride.

"Now, I need to get ready for bed. It's been a long day, and embarrassment takes a lot out of a person."

"Noted. I'll, uh... make us an appointment before I leave for the tour."

He nods in response.

～

TWENTY-FOUR HOURS ISN'T a long time. Not really. But it feels like eternity when you are waiting for test results.

Thank God for my drums, because it has been therapeutic as fuck to bang out my frustrations in rehearsal.

Felix accosts me the second break time hits, but I'm not in the mood.

Well, my cock is, but my brain is spiraling.

No news is good news, right?

Right?

I haven't been tested since before Marci had Bobby. Though Marci and I were faithful to one another, and my bill of health was good then, it has been years.

I shouldn't be so worried, so why am I worried?

"I can't do this right now." I move away from Felix to sit on the couch.

His accent slips. "Are you okay? Did I—"

"No, it's not you. It's me... I..."

Felix plops down next to me, a look of concern coming over his fine features.

"Is this about... the kid?" he asks gingerly.

"Yes and no. It's... we both went and got tested yesterday."

Felix stares at me blankly. "For..."

"I caught him the other night making out with his friend-not boyfriend but probably will be his boyfriend at some point—and I told him he needed to be safe, and we should probably get him tested and—"

"Oh, shit. Wow, that's a lot. I'm sure he's fine, though."

"It's not him I'm worried about," I reply as I look into his eyes with worry.

Felix opens his mouth but no words come out. He blinks. "Are you? Worried you have something?"

The words crush me.

"No. But, you aren't the first, uh... man, I've ever been with."

The words are heavy in the air as Felix nods.

"Who else?" he asks cautiously.

"Issax. 1989."

"How long did that, uh... last?" Felix's voice is featherlight, careful.

"Not long. It was mostly just a *thing* we did once or twice, really, with my wife."

"Oh." Felix nods.

"I mean, it was the eighties, you know," I say quietly. I can see the fear reflected in his pupils, and I want to disappear.

Felix leans closer, his knee sliding between my legs as his bright eyes light up and he offers me a light smile.

"I mean, that was like thirty years ago. I'm sure you're fine," he states.

A pregnant pause forms between us and then he speaks.

"I've been getting tested regularly for a few years. My last test was a couple months ago. Got the all clear, in case you, uh... wanted to know."

I nod. "I mean, it's good to know."

Felix sets his hand on my thigh lightly. "I know this is probably going to sound shitty, but I don't know how else to say it, uh... so bear with me..."

My eyebrows knit together and I worry this is it. He's going to tell me he no longer wants us to continue with...

What, exactly?

What is it that we're doing here?

I know we're fucking around, sort of, but it doesn't feel like fucking around.

It feels... different.

Felix licks his lips, jiggling his lip ring.

"I've never waited this long before. For someone."

My heart sinks at his words.

"Felix, I—"

"But I think... I really fucking like you... and I think you're worth the wait." He closes his eyes, pursing his lips.

I realize as the words leave his lips, they aren't true.

He doesn't *like* me.

And I don't *like* him, either.

I'm falling in love with him.

I pull him close, kissing him with all the fear, the worry, and the pain swirling inside of me.

I pull him closer into my lap and he follows without question. I wrap my arms around his waist, fingers trailing up his back as I press my lips to his. I'm hard within seconds, and so is he, and I have to remember to breathe.

I want him.

I want him so fucking bad it terrifies me.

"I think we need to slow down," I say. Because the emotion swirling in my chest, the words in my throat that long to be known are new and exciting, but also scary.

I look up into his pretty blue eyes, my gaze dipping to his swollen lips, his sliver of metal.

"Right, of course." He nods, swallowing nervously.

"And we need to head back to finish up rehearsal here."

Felix's gaze shifts, and he nods again.

He removes himself from my lap, standing, and straightening his jeans.

"Wait a couple minutes so it's not obvious," he says coolly as he leaves me alone in the dressing room.

CHAPTER 23

F ELIX

W E NEED TO TALK.

I stare at the text, chewing my thumbnail. I know I should ignore it, but when Sully mentions "the cat", I know I can't really ignore it.

And to add extra fuckery to an already souring morning, Samson meows like a damsel in distress.

Please, dad, don't let the big bad asshole take me away! He'll never feed me on time!

I look at Samson with pleading eyes.

"You are so high maintenance, you know that?" I say as I text Sully back with an *okay.*

Bel Air's in an hour work for you?

Of course, he would pick the Bel Air's cafe. He always raved about the place, but I never found their food or their drinks particularly above average.

Fine, I text back.

Truth be told, I don't have much to do, other than pack for the trip. With the concert only four days away, rehearsals are lessening. Once we hit sound check, we should be fine.

And the last couple rehearsals have been damn near flawless.

Duncan's adapted to the material wonderfully, and even Eddie seems to have simmered down a bit. Corpse, too. His playing has always been good, but even I have noticed he's a lot more focused lately.

I have no worries at all about this show.

We're going to fucking *kill* it!

Though, a part of me is annoyed that Sully *assumed* I'd be sitting around my house doing nothing, loafing.

It doesn't matter that he was right, but it pisses me off that he can play off our familiarity, our history together, and irritate the fuck out of me, even when he sounds like he's trying to wave a damn white flag.

Samson meows, a warning.

"I promise," I reassure him, though I'm not sure if he understands me. He is a cat, after all.

When I finally make it to Bel Air's, Sully is sitting outside on the terrace, scrolling his phone.

I notice him slouching, his legs crossed, and he looks disinterested in the world.

He looks up to see me, a wide grin spreading across his face, like he didn't just punch me in my damn face a couple days ago.

He was probably high and doesn't remember, Felix.

"Lixy, so nice of you to come."

"Don't call me that," I bite as I round the table, sliding into a seat across from him.

Sullivan smugly grins. "What the matter, baby? Didn't get your daily dose of dick yet?" he taunts me.

His words are like slime, dripping down a steel wall.

Fucking disgusting.

I cross my legs as a waitress sets down a glass of water in front of me, and a glass of cranberry juice, garnished with lime. I glance at it as she hands Sully a beer.

"What's this?" I ask, even though I know without tasting it, it's a vodka cranberry.

"I thought maybe this meeting would go better if we both took the edge off of things. You're a lot easier to talk to when you don't want to kill me."

I push the drink aside, instead grabbing the water.

"I'm good, thanks."

Sully raises an eyebrow.

"Look at you being all noble and shit. I have to say, it is endearing. Cute almost."

"Cut the shit, Sully. I'll save you some time. I'm keeping the cat."

Sully rolls his eyes.

"Lixy, baby, this isn't about the cat. I just said that so I could get you alone. Surely, you know that. Or has all the alcohol and drugs rotted your brain already?"

I cross my arms, biting my tongue.

I knew this was a bad idea. I knew I shouldn't have come here.

I move to leave. "Well, if that's the case, then my work is done here. There's nothing else to talk about." I get up, making a move for the door.

Sully grabs my wrist, pulling me back.

He presses his thumb into my vein, making me freeze.

"Felix..." his voice is smooth, like whiskey over dry ice.

It makes me forget how to breathe.

Once upon a time, I would have done *anything* for that voice.

That smooth, silky tone that covered me in lies.

I pull my wrist back, glaring at him.

"Don't make me beg," he says darkly and his gaze implores me. "I don't want to fight anymore, baby. I want things to go back to the way they were."

I step back, blinking furiously. I can't have heard him correctly.

He wants me *back?*

"I want back in the band. In the family," he says. "You know, we both have a tendency to get a little..." He runs his finger down my forearm and I shudder. "Hot headed sometimes. Say shit we don't mean."

"I meant everything I said," I remind him. "Drunk or sober."

Sully smugly chortles as he shrugs. "These last couple days, this last week... fuck I've missed you, Felix. I've missed your foul little mouth, your fight." He takes a step closer to me, and I am acutely aware of his proximity.

"I don't miss you. In fact, I've been fucking sky high without you to drag me down."

"I don't believe you," he replies.

I am just about to give him the finger when his hand grabs my throat, holding me still and *kisses* me.

The unmistakable snapping of a shutter echoes around us, and I push him away. So hard I almost knock the table over.

"No," I say, loud enough everyone in a five-mile radius can hear. "You are a poison, Sully. And I'm done with your toxic fucking bullshit. You're too late."

"Lixy, baby!" he calls angrily. "Whoever he is, he isn't me!"

I turn around, glaring at him. "You're right, he isn't. He's a fucking man and he's more than you'll ever be."

I hiss as I jump on my bike, speeding past the darkness and into the light once more.

When I pull up to Duncan's driveway, my phone rings. It's been ringing nonstop for twenty minutes. I pull it from my pocket and glance at the screen to see it's Lou.

No doubt he's already dealing with the onslaught of damage control and wants to probably rip me a new asshole, but right now, I don't need Lou freaking out on me.

Because there's only one person who I need to hear from right now.

I knock on the door, and Duncan opens it almost immediately.

"Felix... I just got off the phone with Lou."

"Oh," I say, feeling speechless.

In my head I'd gone over this exact moment on the way here, but now that it is here...

One. Two. Three.

"Can I... come in?" I ask, feeling on the edge of the precipice.

"Of course." Duncan opens the door wider for me to step in.

"What did Lou say?" I ask hesitantly.

Duncan hands me his phone, and I see the text.

Felix fucked up. Again.

This time I won't be able to clean it up.

I look up at Duncan as the truth is revealed.

I scroll to see the TikToks and Reels, the posts he sent Duncan.

Of Sully grabbing me, kissing me.

Of me yelling about my man who is more than he will ever be.

My eyes glass over, and tears beg to fall.

"I'm so sorry," I say as Duncan pulls me close, holding me against his chest.

His scent encapsulates me and I let go.

I wrap my arms around him, holding on for dear life.

"Did you mean what you said?" he asks.

I bury my tears in his shirt, breathing him in like oxygen as I nod furiously.

"Every fucking word," I say as I sniffle.

He lets go of me, heading down the hall.

"You're not mad at me, are you? For what happened?" I ask, following him.

He heads into the workshop, toward a bench where he's got a guitar that is broken up into parts. It's hot, with the fan circulating air, but it smells highly of varnish and wood, and it's comforting on so many levels.

Duncan shrugs. "No, Felix. I'm not mad. I'm just... keeping my hands busy," he says nodding for me to join him. "Polish that for me, will you? It needs to be completely sanded off before I assemble it."

I don't argue with him as I do what he asks, my phone ringing off the hook.

"You should answer him, you know," he suggests.

"I know," I say, sanding off the chipped blue paint. "But I'm not ready to deal with the storm yet." I glance up at him. "I think it was his plan all along. He couldn't destroy me like he used to. So he tried to destroy the only thing left of me he could."

"Yeah, and what's that?" Duncan asks.

"My image," I reply as I rhythmically sand off the chipped paint until there is nothing left but wood.

Until the last bits of what it was disintegrate, leaving forth a blank canvas.

CHAPTER 24

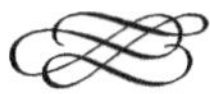

DUNCAN

I LEAVE Felix for a moment to grab us both some waters, when my phone dings.

I pull it out, seeing Lou's string of emojis and worried texts.

Is he with you?

I tap out a yes. There's no point in hiding it.

Lord knows Lou would send out a cavalry if he couldn't find Felix, and I don't want the damn news vans showing up here.

This town is peaceful and removed from Hollywood.

I'd like to keep it that way, for Bobby's sake, but also for Felix's.

And my own.

He's okay. I'll take care of him. Just do what you do best.

Lou types, the bubbles on the screen endless as another text comes through.

Dr. Philenstein's office.

Panic ebbs through me as I swipe, opening the link to the patient portal.

I breathe a sigh of relief when I see my son's clean bill of health.

Thank God.

I still my breath as texts from Lou come through, two in a row.

But for the moment, I have more pressing matters.

I scroll through the same paperwork, my heart in my throat as I settle on the results of my own testing.

All clear.

A huge weight falls off my shoulders and I feel like I could pass out.

Aside from creaky knees, everything is in perfect working condition.

I swallow as the sounds of faint strumming come from down the hall.

Lou texts me.

Tell him I will have a car pick him up at nine. We're going to address this insanity head on, tonight on Romano.

I shoot back a 'k', turning off my phone as I slide it back in my pocket.

I walk down the hall, listening to the faint strums of the guitar, a familiar melody I haven't heard in ages.

I'm surprised Felix knows Frankie Goes To Hollywood's *Power Of Love*, being as it's such an underground track.

But then I think about all the ways Felix keeps surprising me, and how each time, I fall deeper into him, into his powerful vortex.

I stop in the doorway, and he doesn't see me.

He's singing, his accent slipping through, while playing my most recent project.

An acoustic I built myself from reclaimed wood.

The sun shines through the skylight, lighting him up in a golden halo.

His eyelashes are thick, standing out against

his pale skin. He doesn't see me, with his eyes closed.

His voice—his *real* voice—isn't raspy and throaty.

It's softer, deeper.

I watch as he gets lost in his playing, as his fingers dance along the frets, strumming the strings delicately, singing the words with more feeling than anything he's recorded.

And I realize all at once as he sings those spellbinding words, that somewhere between fight and fury, between attitude and obedience, between music and lyrics, I have fallen in love with Felix Hart.

I push off the doorframe, heading toward where he sits, lost in his playing, in the power of the music.

And then I do something I haven't done in a long time.

I sing, too.

Felix's eyes flash open with surprise, but his fingers continue to strum as his voice falters. I continue as he plays, and he joins in until our voices dance together, echoing off the walls.

He stands, slowly walking toward me as he

continues to play, his accent coloring the words with a realness that takes my breath away.

In this business, talent can be manufactured at the drop of a hat, especially today.

But beneath all the tattoos and the attitude, Felix Hart has real, raw talent.

Of course he does.

As I sing out the last line of the song, those final notes ringing out, I know without a doubt, he's paradise.

"Sorry, I, uh... didn't mean to impose on your stuff." He says the words softly.

I take the guitar from his hands carefully, setting it on the workshop table before turning back to him. His blue eyes glitter like diamonds in the setting sunlight.

"Leave a musician in a room full of instruments, what do you expect?" I flash him with a smirk, setting my hands on his hips. I slide one over his left side and he *falls* into me without much guidance.

He stares up at me through his lashes, his tongue jiggling his lip ring as his eyes glaze over.

"Lou finally stopped texting me, I think."

My lips twist up in the corners and I lean

closer, my mouth inches from his. I back him up against the edge of my workshop table.

His gaze darkens as he grows hard against me, biting his lip.

"That's because I told him I'd take care of you," I inform him. "And I may have promised him, I'd have you delivered to Romano tonight."

Felix chews his lower lip, his shoulders loosening as I reach my right hand up his neck, grabbing him just enough to remind him I've got him.

Now, and probably forever.

Because there's no way I'm letting him go.

I don't know how I thought I could fight something like this.

The Power of Love, indeed.

"Typical Lou. Always trying to get ahead of shit," he says. "Will you... will you come with me?" His voice is small, needy.

I use my thumb to tilt his throat up, forcing him to look at me. My cock throbs against him, and I look him in his eyes when I tell him, yes.

And then I press my lips to his.

Felix sinks into me like ink in paper.

Like he was made for me.

I kiss him with renewed confidence, and relief.

I devour him with my whole damn soul.

Our lips part just a bit and I whisper to him, "Results came in."

Felix's gaze simmers as he glances down to my lips, his chest heaving with breath.

"I take it it was good news," he says, flashing me with a smirk.

"Very." I nod, then take his lower lip in my mouth, biting at the flesh.

"Duncan, I—" The way he says my name is like a wish, a prayer.

I slide my fingers over his waist, deftly working at the buttons of his jeans. I hold his gaze, watching the way his pupils dilate.

"Yes, Felix?" I whisper as I feather my mouth over his jaw, a smile curling on my lips.

His heavy breath echoes in the space between us.

"I..." His voice falters, shaking with nerves and I stop.

I look at him, for a moment worried I'm pushing him too much.

He slides both his hands up the side of my neck, licking his kiss-swollen lips.

"I love you." He says the words as if he's terrified, and I realize he *is.*

Because Felix has never loved out loud.

But I will never force him to hide.

Because I don't want to hide, either.

"I know," I say as I crush my lips to his, resuming my onslaught of un-pantsing him.

Felix's hands slid down my neck, the unmistakable look of vulnerability crossing his beautiful face.

"Can I tell you a secret?" I ask, pressing my lips to the underside of his ear,

Felix's hands wander to my jeans and he has my pants down around my ankles in seconds, and is tugging at my shirt.

I chuckle as he breathlessly sighs, "Yeah?"

I slowly tug at the hem of his shirt, and he removes it without question as I do the same, stepping out of my pants.

I'm acutely aware of how the light shines on his naked form and how his tattoos blend with shadows, accentuating his slender, pale form.

"You are so fucking beautiful," I whisper, and Felix crumples in my grasp.

But I won't let him fall.

I let my hands wander over his sinuous form, using my thumb to flick his underside piercing.

"You really think so?" he asks, his accent coloring his words with a sweetness that makes me melt.

I lift him up, and he doesn't miss a beat, wrapping his legs around me. His wet cock slides against my abdomen, making my own ache, and I don't think twice about what I do next.

I carry Felix over to the couch on the other side of the room and carefully lower us both. He arches his back, his leg sliding down my side as he gets comfortable.

I trace my fingers along his infinity tattoo, biting at his lip ring and he groans.

My cock settles at the edge of his entrance, and I wait for his permission. Felix slides his hands down my sides, over my ass, right over my black cat tattoo, and his grip isn't forceful.

It's the lightest of touches, almost as if he is afraid I'll change my mind.

"Are you sure?" he asks, his glassy sapphire pools glistening with so much love, it's impossible to fight.

"I meant what I said to Lou. I promise, I'll take care of you," I whisper.

Felix's gaze holds mine.

"Wait here," I tell him and he blinks as I extricate myself from him for a moment, heading to the ensuite bathroom.

When I come back with the bottle of lube, I can't help but appreciate the sight of Felix, spread on my couch, naked, with his cock in his hand, looking up at me like he did from the pages of Playgirl.

"Are you sure?" I ask, popping the cap off.

One. Two. Three.

Felix strokes himself, showing off his sparkling steel barbell.

He bites his lip as he nods. "I told you, I don't mind being fucked."

I shake my head, rubbing lube between my fingers first, tossing the bottle on the cushions next to him.

Four. Five. Six.

I stalk closer to him, and he grins.

"I'm not going to fuck you, Felix," I say and he frowns.

I settle between his legs, lifting them onto my shoulders, pushing him back into the couch.

I slide my tongue along his shaft, flicking over his piercing as I slowly breach his hole with my lubed finger, and he cries out immediately with a deep groan.

I continue my onslaught slowly, stretching him as I lick his cock.

He squirms beneath me. "Please..." He writhes, begging with that saccharine desperation that has me unable to deny him.

I slide another finger in, and he grabs my head, fingers gripping my locks as he attempts to face fuck me.

I stroke my tongue along his piercing as I pull my fingers out and he curses.

"I told you, I'm not going to fuck you," I bite as I grab the lube, taking my time as I apply it to his twitching hole, then to my throbbing cock.

Felix gazes up at me, and I keep my sights set on those pretty sapphires.

I press my cockhead against his entrance, and he holds my gaze.

I lean forward just the slightest, gripping the back of the couch with my fingers as I inch myself in slowly. The only sounds that can be heard is our heavy, labored breathing.

"I'm going to make love to you, Felix Hart. Do you understand?"

Felix swallows harshly, nodding wordlessly as

I take his lips with mine. His right hand grabs my neck as his left grabs my ass. He pulls me forward, and I bottom out.

Brat.

I slide my tongue in his mouth as I pull my hips back.

He's so *tight*. I don't know if I'll be able to make it. But I have to try.

I grab his wrists, forcing them up by his head.

He wraps his legs around me, ankles locking as his cock leaves sticky trails of precum against my abdomen.

"Because I love you, too." I whisper the words against his lips and the smallest sound of submission escapes his throat.

"Do you understand?" I ask, biting his lip as his hips meet my thrust.

He nods hazily, breathing out, "Yes".

I lose myself in the motion, the rhythm of my thrusts, the sound of slapping skin and breathy moans, and the feeling of being tangled up in Felix Hart.

And when he comes undone beneath me, I know my fate is sealed.

My heart is no longer an empty shell.

I'm no longer hollow.

CHAPTER 25

Felix

I WAKE up in Duncan's bed, but the last thing I remember is being in his workshop. I rub my eyes, my vision sharpening as he pulls on a pair of pants.

"What time is it?" I ask.

I move slightly, and my thighs... and ass, feel sore as hell.

But, God, was it fucking worth it.

Better than I fantasized about, that's for sure.

I stare at Duncan in the low light, appreciating the sight.

Then the door opens, and there is a scream.

I turn to see the owner of the pipes, and realize it's Bobby.

Fuck.

"What the hell, don't you knock?" Duncan yips, and I pull the covers up as if that's going to hide my naked ass, but I'm in his fucking bed.

You don't have to be a math genius to put two and two together.

"Oh, so the open door policy doesn't include you?" Bobby snarks.

"Bobby..." Duncan sighs.

"This is the guy?" Bobby says with a screech.

Duncan is flustered, gruffly pulling on his shirt and I watch the two of them, feeling like all I want to do is disappear into this mattress.

"Yes," Duncan replies, running his hand over his face.

Bobby's eyes widen.

I think he's going to say something, maybe freak out, but instead, Bobby looks between us and says, "This makes us even, now. Well, this and an extra ticket to the show. Please."

Duncan raises an eyebrow, his jaw tense.

"You, your aunt, and..."

"Done," I say with a shrug.

"Brendan. Duh."

I raise my hand, but nobody acknowledges me. "Who's Brendan?"

"His friend," Duncan bites at the same time Bobby says, "My boyfriend."

Oh.

Oh.

Shit.

"And a car." Bobby crosses his arms, raising an eyebrow at his father.

"Absolutely not!" Duncan bites, shooing him out of the room. "Ticket, fine. Car no."

I hear them talking as Bobby whines, but relents, and I can't help but laugh.

I seem to do a lot of that around Duncan, and I get the feeling that will never change.

But hey, if I can handle being caught bare-assed by my boyfriend's kid, surely, I can handle telling the world I'm gay and in love with my drummer, right?

Right?

～

LOU SMOOTHES out Duncan's shirt, his jaw tense.

"Are you sure about this?" he asks.

Duncan stands tall, which isn't difficult. "I'm sure."

Lou looks at me, shaking his head. "And you? You sure this... is worth it? For you?"

I nod, my voice serious. "If Ghost can choke each other on stage and ignite a hundred fanfics, I'm sure we'll be just fine."

Duncan raises an eyebrow.

"You do know who Ghost is, right?" I ask, and he shakes his head.

"I'm starting to wonder if you are worth all this trouble," I tease.

Duncan glares at me, his lip twitching.

Which is exactly what I want.

Punish me, Daddy, please, please, please.

"All right, five minutes, guys. Take your places," a staffer says as Romano waves at us.

Lou sighs. "Then I got your back. Both of you. Now, let's break the fucking Internet. Or whatever the kids say."

Duncan turns to look at me, giving me a soft smile.

One. Two. Three.

"That's low even for you."

Four. Five. Six.

I shrug, haughtily grinning at him, feeling like for the first time in my life I don't have to worry about a thing.

Seven. Eight. Nine.

Because as long as Duncan is by my side, I know I can handle any storm.

"It's show time," Lou says as Romano announces me.

I slide my hand into Duncan's and he holds it tightly.

Ten.

I walk out among the lights, my hand in his, for all the world to see, as we take our seats.

ONE WEEK Later

Duncan

"DID YOU PACK YOUR TOOTHBRUSH?" Bobby asks as I zip up my duffel.

"Yes, Bobby, I packed *two.*"

"Okay, what about your—"

"I have it under control," I reply as Bobby huffs in annoyance.

The doorbell rings, and Bobby rolls his eyes as he heads to open it.

I set my duffel next to my suitcase by the door.

"Hey, Felix." Bobby leaves the door open as he heads back into the kitchen, hip checking me. "Your boyfriend's here," he taunts me.

I shoot him a glare.

"That reminds me... rules still apply while I'm gone. I'll be checking in with your Aunt Maria. Daily."

Bobby scoffs at me, twisting his lips. "Mhmm. Same rules apply for you, too, you know. I'll be checking in with Lou to make sure you stay out of trouble."

I laugh, and he smiles.

Only I know it's not an empty threat.

The kid does not need more ammo for a car.

I've already had to dissuade Felix twice from *gifting* him one for his birthday next month.

It took a lot of convincing, but I was very persuasive.

Felix grabs my suitcase and duffel, and I move to stop him, but he waves me off.

"Wouldn't want the old man to throw his back out before we leave the parking lot." He flashes me with a wicked grin.

"I'll give you something to throw your fucking back out," I bite.

Maria comes out from the guest room to stand beside Bobby, who is shaking his head.

Felix nods at Bobby. "I'll take good care of him, don't worry."

Bobby's shoulders fall, and he heads toward us. He hugs Felix, whose eyes widen in surprise.

"Promise," he demands.

Felix slowly wraps his arms around my kid, and my heart melts.

I know this, a real relationship, let alone with a single dad, is not easy for him, and the future is full of challenges. But I've always embraced a challenge, and if there's one thing I've learned about Felix Hart, it is that he is a fighter.

And he's most certainly worth a hundred Callahans.

"Promise, kid," he says softly, looking at me.

"I'll, uh... take these to the car," he says. He

lets Bobby go, taking my luggage, leaving Bobby and me in the living room.

"I'm going to go start unpacking," Maria says, meeting my gaze with a soft smile of her own.

I know she doesn't understand this new familial development, but I'm thankful she's supportive, nonetheless.

Marci would want you to be happy, so if you're happy, that's all that matters.

Her words echo in my brain, and I look at my son, with glassy eyes.

My throat is tight as I feel anxiety swelling.

I'm going to miss him so fucking much.

I pull him into a hug and he doesn't fight me.

He grabs onto me, a small sob tearing from his throat.

"No fights while I'm gone, okay?" I say, my voice shaking.

Bobby nods, his tears soaking my shirt.

"It's only a couple months, kiddo. I'll be back before you know it."

I hold him in front of me and he wipes his eyes.

"I know," he says, stepping away from me.

One. Two. Three.

I take one step at a time until I'm out the door.

Four. Five. Six.

I climb onto the first step of the bus, turning around to see Bobby on the front porch, waving with a grin.

Seven. Eight. Nine.

I ascend the steps, turning the corner as the doors close.

Lou smiles. "Welcome back, McKay. Let's get this show on the road"

I find Felix lounging on the bus couch, petting a... cat?

"What is that?" I ask.

Felix glances up at me.

"This is Samson."

"You didn't tell me you had a cat," I say as I take a seat next to him, kicking my feet up on top of my duffel.

Felix raises an eyebrow. "Are you allergic to cats?" He asks as Samson looks at me.

I shake my head. "No. I've always liked pussy," I taunt him.

Felix haughtily purrs, his lip ring dancing as he plays with it.

"Well, this pussy needs to be fed at five am

every day or he will murder you in your sleep. And he gets treats twice a day."

I chuckle at his bratty tone. "Fine. Pain in my ass."

Samson leaps down from Felix's lap, curling up in a little coffin-shaped pet bed.

"Is that a threat, Duncan?" Felix asks, his voice edged with darkness.

"Guess you'll just have to wait and see," I tease as I pick up the blue guitar I gave him.

The one he helped me build.

I strum out a few familiar notes, and Felix doesn't miss a beat. He taps out a rhythm along my thigh, singing the lyrics to *Lovin' On The Run*, and I can't help but smile.

Because as we head off into the California sunset, toward our next city, I know the best song has yet to be written.

Thank you for reading Hollow Heart!
Continue with the next book in the Rock His World series, Wild Stars.

IF YOU ENJOYED THIS BOOK, maybe you'll do me a huge favor and leave a review. Even a few words would mean the world to me, and it also helps other readers find the stories you love.

THANKS!

~Evie Riley

Rock His World

Hollow Heart

Wild Stars

Grave Misgivings

Federal Protection Agency

Mason

Rafe

Ryzen

Cooper

Noah

Damien

Sebastian

Gabe

Logan

Ruthless Empire

Courting Danger

Chasing Danger

Kissing Danger

Smokejumpers

Hawke

Cyrus

Jase

Gage

Jackson

Xavier

Jasper Springs

Cade

Dawson

Drew

Grayson

Riley

Mitch

From The Edge

Shattered

Runaway

Jaded

Rescue

Hidden

Tormented

Gray Vale Pack

His Fated Mate

His Wounded Warrior

His Healing Heart

ABOUT THE AUTHOR

Evie Riley is a prolific, neurodivergent author known for her captivating MM romance novels. She has gained a significant following and topped the LGBT+ action and adventure bestseller charts with her series.

Evie's writing style often explores dark and gritty themes where her men must overcome difficult obstacles in their search for love, but she has also ventured into sweeter small-town romances, incorporating tropes like enemies-to-lovers, friends-to-lovers, age-gap, and forced proximity. She is known for crafting engaging romantic suspense novels and has a knack for creating interconnected series worlds that keep readers invested.

Outside of writing, she enjoys spending time at the beach and has a quirky personality, described by her partner as ranging from cute to deadly, depending on her blood-chocolate levels.

Evie spends her nights writing bad boys in love, and her days wrangling the sweet boys she loves.

www.ingramcontent.com/pod-product-compliance
Lightning Source LLC
Chambersburg PA
CBHW061056210726
48294CB00001B/173